Eat No Evil

Also by Frank Dewey Staley:

Ocracoke
A novel

Saving Women
A collection of short stories

Orphans
A novel

Eat No Evil

Frank Dewey Staley

EAT NO EVIL

iUniverse books may be ordered through booksellers or by contacting:

iUniverse
1663 Liberty Drive
Bloomington, IN 47403
www.iuniverse.com
844-349-9409

Because of the dynamic nature of the Internet, any web addresses or
links contained in this book may have changed since publication and
may no longer be valid. The views expressed in this work are solely those
of the author and do not necessarily reflect the views of the publisher,
and the publisher hereby disclaims any responsibility for them.

Any people depicted in stock imagery provided by Getty Images are
models, and such images are being used for illustrative purposes only.
Certain stock imagery © Getty Images.

ISBN: 978-1-6632-3695-1 (sc)
ISBN: 978-1-6632-3696-8 (e)

Print information available on the last page.

iUniverse rev. date: 03/14/2022

To Anne and Ellen

Don't you know yet? It's your light that lights the world.
Jalaluddin Rumi
Sufi Poet

Millie and Edward

Edward Chase had not spoken to his wife in three days. Blessed with a supremely high level of intelligence and a superior memory, he couldn't seem to remember what triggered this latest installment of silence. Not that he devoted much time or energy in trying to do so. He had actually developed a sense of comfort in the distance and silence that existed between them. And it was no worse than any of the instances preceding this. But he was smart enough to know that this was not sustainable in any sense of a relationship. Especially with someone he loved so passionately.

She was sitting in a large reclining chair in the living room blessed with a splendid view of the fourth hole of the Twin Oaks Golf and Country Club. She wore a pair of baggy jeans and a red tank top. Her feet were bare. Her legs were bent so that her knees touched her chin. She was reading a book perched at the top of her knees. She did not look up.

He climbed the stairs and entered the bedroom that had become his alone. Millie had taken up residence on the sofa in the living room. Edward knew a great deal about human emotion; he understood the dynamic of crossing battle lines. He also knew the courage and humility it took to take the first step back toward normality. He loved his wife, and he knew he would be the one to do this. He would not allow indifference to take hold of him. At least not now.

He changed out of his slacks and dress shirt, tossing his tie on the bed. He dressed in his after-work and weekend uniform: shorts, loose-fitting tee shirt and sandals. He hung his slacks in the closet and tossed the shirt and his socks into a hamper.

"I'm going for a walk," he said as he went to the kitchen sink to get a glass of water. He could not see Millie from this vantage point, but their voices easily carried from room to room.

She didn't respond.

Edward leaned into the living room.

"Mill, this is nutso. I know you're mad. I know I've disappointed you. But we have to step back across the line. I love you. Please come for a walk with me. Let's talk."

She placed her book on the small table beside her chair. Before standing, she straightened her legs out in front of her. She possessed long and very shapely legs. The dark red polish on her toenails had weathered and chipped.

"Alright," she said, "but you're going first."

Edward and Millie Chase lived on a cul-de-sac carved exactly one mile into the golf course. None of the homes were more than five years old. They were constructed just differently enough in their design to look uniformed. This was one of the more upscale neighborhoods in Botetourt, Virginia, but its houses did not approach ostentation. The verdant beauty of the golf course enhanced the views. Further out, the horse farms built on the rolling hills circling the village, with miles and miles of dark-painted fences, made this a much sought-after place to live.

They walked toward the main road, Edward on the sidewalk, Millie on the lawns of their neighbors. She had not worn shoes. They intersected three driveways before he said anything.

"We can't keep having the same discussion. It's not healthy, and the stakes will keep going up."

"Don't give me a lot of your psychiatrist bullshit, okay, Edward?"

"I'm just pointing out the obvious, Mil. I hear you when you talk to me, and I'm sensitive to how you feel. And I think there are things we could do, steps we could take together to find some common ground."

"If you understand me," she said, "if you understand how I feel, then what are we doing living here? Why do you keep bugging me to have another baby?"

And it was out and, in the air, once again. Their discussions that seemed now to always devolve into arguments and painful silences resulted from the idea of having a child.

They walked on in silence to the end of the cul-de-sac and turned back toward home.

They had met while both were attending Elmira College in upstate New York. Millicent Lee was the oldest of three daughters in a very well-to-do, first-generation Korean family from Indianapolis. Her senior year in high school she attended a week-long seminar for gifted artists held at the Delacroix School of the Arts in New York City. A young woman from somewhere on Long Island shared her classes at Delacroix, and the two quickly became close friends. When Abby Lowe decided to go to Elmira the next year, it only made sense that Millie would join her. Elmira College benefitted from the pipeline of eighteen year-old girls streaming in from well-off families from towns and cities sprinkled throughout Long Island. It was well known to be a bastion of the upscale. Horses were ridden; field hockey was played. The school was also known to turn a blind eye when an applicant's test scores or grade point average did not meet the minimum requirements. The administration governing Elmira College valued quality education. To a person, however, they knew how the bills were paid.

And this was the reason, four years before Millicent Lee arrived on campus, that Elmira College began to accept male students. The stream of young women from Long Island to central New York State had slowed to a trickle. New blood and new revenue streams were needed.

In came the young men over the next several years, among them Edward Chase. His was not a wealthy family; Edward's parents could not have afforded the tuition nor the room and board. Back in Watertown, a small town not far from the Canadian border in northern New York, his father had made a decent living as a grocery store manager. His mother worked part-time as a secretary at the elementary school. As a high school senior, Edward seemed destined for community college and state university. But he was an exceptional student, graduating near the top of his class. He was also a very much better-than-average basketball player on a team that went to the state finals. This combination of attributes spoke to the admissions office at Elmira College. They were always looking to lend a hand to students possessed of high scholastic achievement. And their basketball team, only two years in existence, needed good players. The day he got the letter offering him a scholarship he had to look on a map to find the place.

"Where you from?"

"Are you asking me that because I'm Asian?" said Millicent

The young man with dark hair and blue eyes smiled.

"Not at all. That would be rude. I'm asking because I think you're new here. A school this small, you get to know everybody. I haven't seen you around before."

"I'm from Indiana. This is my first year."

"I'm Edward," he said as he extended his hand.

"I'm Millicent. Well, Millie," she said. "It's very nice to meet you."

They were at a small gathering at a fellow-student's apartment. Of the dozen or so people in the assorted circles of conversation, they had taken notice of each other from across the room. Edward was a head taller than anyone around him, and he moved with gestures that spoke of confidence. Millie was the only non-Caucasian. He possessed an air of authority; she was strikingly beautiful.

Her hair was long in those days, with bangs cut straight across her forehead just above the eye line. She was tall and thin; her hands seemed like those of a concert pianist. Her nails were short and uneven. Her knuckles were red and raw.

But Edward noticed her eyes. Dark and bright, kindness and evil in equal dimensions.

"What're you going to study, Millie?"

"Art History," she said. "You?"

"Chemistry," he said. "They don't really have a pre-med program here, so that's the next best thing."

They stood together and sipped beer out of paper cups for most of that first encounter. Millie learned that Edward was a jock, but a genuinely brilliant jock. She liked his tendency toward legitimate self-deprecation; most people willing to poke fun at themselves were actually doing it in an effort to highlight something or other in their makeup. She knew this, and this was not Edward.

And Edward learned that Millie was unpretentious. She was as confident as any young woman he had ever met. She didn't need to show anyone that she was a person of substance. She didn't smile on cue unless something amused her; she maintained eye contact even when she spoke.

The on and off romance remained mostly on over the next couple of years. While unsettled with each other, each had dated other people. But the magnetism that had attracted them to one another was cellular; it faded, but never seemed to go away entirely. In the end, the attraction could not be ignored. Even while apart at great distances, each seemed to sense the other in close proximity.

Edward learned that he had been accepted to medical school while spending Christmas at Millie's home in Indianapolis. His mother had called and had opened the notification letter while on the phone with her son.

"Thank you," he said to the woman who had raised him. "I love you, too. Yup. Merry Christmas to you, as well."

He was standing with his back to the counter-top island in the middle of the Lee's large kitchen. Millie stood at the sink washing potatoes, her long and slender back to him.

"How's your mom?" she asked without turning around.

"Good. She sends her love."

"That's nice," said Millie.

"And I got into med school. Rochester. That's why she called."

Millie Lee did not allow the thought that she had two years of school remaining while the man she loved would be leaving in a few months to cross her mind. She did not, in fact, think of herself at all. Not even for an instant.

She turned from the sink and went to him, the water still running. She jumped into his arms, straddling his waist as he held her up, one hand on each butt cheek. She kissed him on each corner of his mouth. He could feel her hands, wet and cold, on the back of his neck, and he loved her as completely in that moment as he would ever love anyone in his life.

"I am so fucking proud of you," she whispered.

His was a family of seriously-minded people. They studied hard; they played their sports hard. They had profound work ethic. They competed intensely and were stoic in victory and defeat. They loved each other as most families do, but over-the-top reactions were not in their genetic codings.

"That's the first time anybody's said that to me," he whispered back.

He held on and didn't lower her to ground for several seconds. It was warm and electric and sexual and fulfilling. She felt all of these things. And she could feel his breathing and his shoulders climbing and falling as he wept for the first time in his adult life.

They made it a year. The drive from Elmira to Rochester was not daunting, but a trip turned routine of any distance gets old. Every weekend became every-other weekend which became once a month. They had holidays. They spent Christmas with the Lees in Indianapolis. It was becoming a tradition, and Millie's parents almost demanded it.

"I want to marry you," said Edward.

They were sitting on the sofa in the Lee's living room. It was dark except for the green and blue tree lights. Millie's legs draped over his thighs as they sat half-facing each other.

"I don't mean right now," he continued. "I don't even mean in the imminent future. But soon, I think. Maybe when I get out of med school."

"God, Edward, could you be any less romantic? You're making it sound like you're planning a surgery or something."

She could see him smile in the darkness.

"You're the person I want to be with. I have a difficult time thinking about my life without you in it."

"That's a little better," she said. "And I love you, too."

On the drive back to Elmira, where Edward's car had been parked, they made the plan to spend the Summer together. Through the school, Edward had secured a job as an orderly at the teaching hospital.

"Change bedpans, wheel patients around from place to place. You know, the shit nobody else really wants to do."

"I could get a job waitressing, or maybe as a clerk in some store," she said.

"It will be very nice to be together again," he said as he drove Millie's Honda sedan north through the state of Pennsylvania.

That Summer became the rest of their lives. They lived in a third floor converted attic. Their landlords, two floors down, had made the renovations to accommodate their own adult children many years earlier. The tiny apartment had large dormers cut into opposite sides of the sloped walls. The brightness of the sunlight warmed the room on days when chilly air flowed in from Lake Ontario.

It was change for Millie. She had been raised in the new world, a combination of formal and formulated daughter of Asian parents and rich girl who merely needed to ask for life's pleasantries. Keeping a house, even a small semblance of a house, was not in her comfort zone.

Their comfort level with one another, however, was profound. Neither of them possessed an ounce of cooking ability, and the level of honesty expressed upon each tasting proved this.

"This may be the worst thing I've ever put in my mouth," she said.

The dinner he had prepared was meant to have been some sort of curry-infused chicken dish. The chicken was over-cooked to the point of near liquid form. The sauce was clearly of curry in nature, but hinted, very strongly, of fuel oil. The texture was gelatinous.

"Don't hold back, Mil. I mean, we're not going to get good at this unless we go through the trial and error process. I can take it."

She stood on her toes and kissed him.

"Well, that was clearly both of those. Good try, but an error, my love. Come on. I'll buy you a hamburger."

The money Millie made working at a coffee shop was enough to pay the rent and power bill. Edward put groceries on the table.

"How are you going to make ends meet when I'm gone?" she asked two weeks before her semester was to begin.

"I get my scholarship cash...not that that's going to make a huge difference. And I'm taking out a loan. Not much, but enough to probably get by. I'll be fine."

They walked along the lakeshore. It was overcast with a high sky and chilly for August, even in northern New York. Millie wore expensive hiking boots, Edward a pair of broken down basketball shoes.

"I know what you're thinking," he said.

"No, you don't."

"You're feeling sorry for me. You're worried that I might not be able to make ends meet. That I'll suffer from malnutrition. That I'll have to sell pints of blood to buy food."

"Not even close."

"And you're thinking that you could give me some of your savings. You know, rich girl helping out destitute student boyfriend kind of thing?"

"God, you're such a know-it-all. But you're not even in the ballpark. What I was thinking is that I could stay. I don't want to invite myself, but I guess I just did. I could stay and finish my degree later."

Intelligent people, and Edward Chase was very certainly a poster child of that group, recognize moments of definition in life as they come across them. He and Millie had spoken of this. The trial run comprised of the Summer just spent together was a blinding success. Both sets of parents, in very different ways, were conservative and traditional. That being said, this was the late 70's. Young people took living together out of wedlock as an often necessary and prudent step before marriage. The parents would approve, albeit with closed-mouth smiles.

"What'll your folks say about quitting school?"

"I'm not quitting. I'm taking a break. A sabbatical. I'll finish it later."

"Aren't you worried about the interruption? A lot of students do that and never get focused enough to go back."

She broke stride and took hold of his arm, turning him until they faced each other. The wind off the water was coming up.

"Edward, it's an undergraduate degree in Art History. It's not going anywhere. There will always be people like me. Artsy, somewhat impractical people who want to study that stuff. I *will* finish. Just not now. If you don't want me to stay, just say so."

She released his arm, and they began walking again. They listened to the waves breaking beneath the path and the ever-present squawking from gulls hovering overhead. These silences had never been signs of alarm, nor were they uncomfortable. Each recognized the other's space for breathing and contemplation.

Fifty yards later, Edward took Millie's arm and turned her toward him.

"We're going to need a bigger bed," he said. "That one was okay for a couple months, but it won't do if you're staying."

She turned and continued the walk.

"Good call," she said.

Millie did not go back to school. She fought her way through the painful conversation with her parents, left Elmira

College and moved in to the third floor attic apartment in Rochester with Edward.

"I promise you I'll get my degree," she had told her father.

"People in our family don't do this," he had said.

She grabbed up as many hours at the coffee shop as she could get. Never having had to worry about money... emergency infusions of cash were always a simple phone call to Indianapolis away...she was now the major earner in their household.

Edward ground away at his second year of med school, and then his third. This is how they measured time, by semesters and years until med school would be complete and Edward could earn a moderately comfortable income as a resident. In April of that year Millie informed him that she was pregnant. Theirs had been a fiery and frequent sex life, with contraception almost an afterthought. She preferred not to take the pill, was squeamish about IUD's and almost indifferent to the diaphragm her doctor had given her. It was messy and usually never left the underwear drawer where she stored it. During the several days each month of high conception risk, Edward pulled out.

They had enjoyed a rare Sunday morning of neither of them having to work or study. Coffee and fresh cinnamon rolls for breakfast, followed by a leisurely stroll along the lakefront.

"We've always seemed to have our big conversations on this path," she said.

"What news do you have for me, Millie. Would you like me to propose to you?"

She took a deep breath. Her stride remained unchanged. Her focus stayed in front of her.

"It might be something for us to consider, Edward. I'm going to have a baby."

He took this announcement in stride. He made a quick mental note of how she had told him. She didn't tell him that she was pregnant. She told him that she was having a baby. If there were decisions to be made, he suspected quite accurately that she had already made them.

He stopped and faced her. Her shoulders in his hands, he turned her to him and looked at her dark, dark eyes. She did not blink.

"I guess we need to start thinking of a proper name."

At this point he detected, but just barely, the smile that came to her closed mouth. Millie, he knew, could be moody. She had a disposition toward despondency that he knew to be clinical, but mild, depression. He knew better than to assume that it was his responsibility to make her happy, to keep her on an even keel. All the same, it elated him when he was able to contribute to her happiness, even when this happiness was manifested by only a tiny and momentary smile.

The marriage was a slapdash affair back in Indianapolis at the end of his semester six weeks later. Attendance was limited to both sets of parents as well as the limited assortment of siblings, aunts and uncles able to travel on such short notice. It was a lovely ceremony conducted by a unitarian minister in a rented wing of an upscale hotel in the downtown area. A pricey and well-known steakhouse around the corner catered the reception. A string quartet from the University of Indianapolis provided the entertainment. As Millie danced with her father, she asked if he was disappointed in her.

"This road we travel in life is long, Millicent," he said. "I love you and I am happy that you have married such a fine young man. You may disappoint me at some point in your life, but that time is not now. I'm proud of the woman you are."

Edward and Millie stayed in a room at the hotel, a gift from her parents. The next morning, a Sunday, they headed back to Rochester in Millie's Honda. She was due at the coffee shop early Monday morning.

Life truly did not change substantially. Edward's hectic and often changing schedule left him with only small slices of down-time. Millie continued to pick up extra hours at the coffee shop.

Marriage had really only altered their lifestyles in one way, but it was a notable alteration. Now that Millicent Lee was a married woman, and especially now that she was a married woman expecting a child, the cool air that had existed between herself and her parents began to warm. As stoic and almost detached as Edward's parents could be, Millie's were expansive and open. Trucks arrived on a near weekly basis delivering boxes filled with baby clothes, towels and assorted toys. As often as not, a box might contain a check for a hundred dollars made out to Millicent Chase. The newly-wed couple's days of near poverty were over, and they both knew they had the baby to thank for that.

"Do you know if it's a boy or a girl?" asked her mother.

Injie Lee was a stylish, yet matronly woman. She dressed in fine clothes and drove a Mercedes. She had come to America with her parents as a little girl. She had been a dutiful child and had grown into a firm but loving mother.

She doted on her husband, as her mother had doted on her father. She lived for her family and now, as her first grandchild was on its way to her, she walked with a lighter step and spoke with a more melodious timbre to her voice.

"We don't want to know," said Millie.

The women had grown closer, and now spoke regularly on the phone. Millie was not enamored of sharing any intimacies with anyone in her life, particularly her mother. But the boxes of baby goodies and checks kept coming, so she figured it was the least she could do.

"Millicent, how can I know what to get? Blue or pink?"

Millie was more lying than sitting at the dinner table in what Edward referred to as the west wing of their attic apartment. She wore a yellow peasant dress…the kind of loose-fitting frock hippie girls in the 60's used to wear. Her bare feet rested on the tabletop. Her belly, always tight as a newly made bedspread, had grown significantly as she inched toward her eighth month of pregnancy.

"Mother, I love the gifts. I really do. But you're already spoiling this child before its even born, you know?"

"How's Edward?"

Injie Lee was deferential to her husband in all matters. But with her girls, her decisions and opinions were the ones that ruled the day. She dismissed her daughter's concern about spoiling her soon-to-be-born grandchild as if she were swatting away a mosquito. The immediate change of subject made this abundantly clear to her daughter.

"Busy, of course. But doing very well. He's near the top of his class with everything her does. And he dotes on me relentlessly. I'm a very lucky woman that I'm married to him. Did you know that he brings me flowers every Friday night?

Even if we're broke and he can only afford one, he brings me something."

"He's the lucky one," said her mother. "How are you feeling?"

"A little tired. I'm glad I don't have to work as much. Thank you for sending those checks. They're lifesavers."

"Your father will be home soon. I have to start his dinner. I love you. Take care of yourself. Bye."

"Bye, mother."

This was vintage Lee-family sign-off language. Almost as if the phone bills were calculated by the number of words transmitted over the wires.

Millie hoisted her feet and legs off the table and went to the sink for a glass of water. Her own husband would be home in an hour, and she had planned on making him a chicken breast with fresh carrots. This had become her go-to dish. Light years from being anything close to resembling an accomplished cook when they took up residence together, she had attacked one cookbook after another and was now, by her own reckoning, passable. He offered often to cook, but they agreed that she was better at it.

She threw up the third swallow of water and leaned heavily on the sink as the pain she felt in her abdomen hit her. Her face burned and was instantly covered with a sheen of sweat. Her hair, now longer and tucked behind each ear, had fallen loose and was plastered to her temples.

With baby steps, she inched to the bathroom in the east wing of the attic. She stepped out of her panties and slid them, blood soaked, to the side. Her belly hurt as if she'd been stabbed. She fought back the need to vomit. She had never known terror in her young life. But she knew it now.

As Millie passed further along into the later stages of her pregnancy, she and Edward had begun to live life as if each were one side of a triangle. The baby was real; the baby was one of them. The baby would complete the geometry. And then the baby was gone, as if it had never existed. Millie had been rushed to the hospital by ambulance. Their child, a girl, had lived a matter of minutes after being delivered.

The days and weeks of depression that followed threatened to consume Millie. Through school, Edward was able to arrange for counseling. They attended the weekly sessions together, often sitting side-by-side and holding hands during the unpleasantness of revisiting their loss. He suffered greatly, but not to the degree to which his wife did. It took months before she could leave the apartment by herself; it was almost a year before she returned to work at the coffee shop. As a gift from heaven, most of the staff had turned over. She did not need, nor want condolences. She craved anonymity.

So here was the handsome couple walking the cul-de-sac. It had been a clear day and was now settling into a warm evening. Stars waited to fill up the sky. As a car passed, some neighbor arriving home from work, Edward waved. Millie walked the lawns in her bare feet and her head down.

"I'm sorry I asked about another baby," he said.

"You say that every time, Edward, and then you ask again."

"We're young. I asked again because I thought you'd softened on the idea. I can't remember what it was exactly, but something you did or said made me think that."

"I haven't softened on anything."

"No, wait. You were telling me about the guy at the store carrying his kid all around the place on his shoulders. That it was cute, him pushing the cart with one hand and holding his kid steady on his shoulders the whole time."

"Jesus Christ, Edward. You're a psychiatrist, for heaven's sake. All those years of school and training. All the books, all the seminars. Are you kidding me? Sometimes a guy carrying a kid on his shoulders is just that. It's cute. My pointing that out isn't some deep-seated, cryptic reaction that speaks to wanting to try to have another child. Maybe it's just me sharing something that I thought was nice. You know, Doctor, sometimes a cigar is just a cigar."

"It's been five years, is all. And I don't want to diminish your grief. I have grief, also."

Half-way through his residency Edward brought up the possibility of having another child. He could easily recreate the wondrous sensations of anticipation and excitement that he felt during Millie's pregnancy. He wanted all of it again.

There was also the fact that his wife struggled to deal successfully with the loss of her baby. He knew better than most, at least at a clinical level, that Millie's loss would never completely be unfelt. But he knew that recovery, at least from a mental health perspective, was possible.

Having a child is never a good recipe for solving issues. Couples who believe the addition of a baby will resolve marital problems are rarely right. Deep in his heart, Edward knew that a child was not the elixir Millie might need to finally step out of the shadow of her painful memories. All that said, he wanted to be a father.

The first time he raised the subject was like every time he raised the subject. Rather than fill Millie with a spark of hope, with a tinge of feeling a life potentially growing inside her, it had the opposite effect. The thought of another pregnancy caused her to collapse back within herself. After clearly and unequivocally telling her husband that she had no desire to go through any of that again, she fell into herself for a number of days. She didn't speak. She didn't smile.

Rinse and repeat. Despite the fact that Edward and Millie were extremely intelligent people, despite the fact that they remained very much committed to and in love with each other, nothing changed. The strain on their marriage was absorbable. They rarely argued because, for the most part, they rarely allowed the issue out in the open. But it stayed with both of them. It was a cluster of cells they could not feel but knew resided somewhere inside each of them.

Not that their existence was entirely bleak. In time, they came close to returning to their old selves. They walked the shoreline. They whispered to each other while lying in bed at night. Edward shared experiences he'd had at the hospital's psych ward; Millie continued to work at the coffee shop and to refine her recipes at home. This loss could have, and would have with many other couples, been too much for their relationship to endure. But both of them were from families of substance; the bond of marriage was not only spiritual and emotional. It was practical. It was contractual.

Back from walking the cul-de-sac, Millie went to the kitchen to begin dinner. Edward followed her and sat on a stool at the counter.

"I love you, Mil. I don't want to argue, I really don't, but I want to say something."

He interpreted her silence as a green light.

"I think that this issue needs to be resolved one way or another. And I know that in your mind, it has been resolved. But it hasn't."

"So, will it be resolved when I agree to get knocked up again? Is that the resolution you're looking for, Edward?"

"I don't know," he said. "Maybe we're…maybe you and I are just not able to come to some sort of closure on our own. Maybe we could get some advice. Maybe talk to someone who could lead us to some sort of resolution. I mean, I work in this stuff all day long. It often works. Very intelligent people sometimes just need a little guidance to get stuff settled."

Millie stood opposite him at the counter. She had taken two chicken breasts from the refrigerator and placed them on the cutting board in front of her. She held a large knife. She looked up and made eye contact with her husband for the first time that day. Their blue and brown eye colors intersected somewhere over the chicken. The new color, some indescribable, but not unpleasing shade of the spectrum, lingered. They both saw it and associated comfort with it. But each of them remained unaware that the other had noticed this tiny and fleeting miracle of light and vision.

"Like counseling? Again?" she said.

"Yes. It was helpful to a degree then. Maybe another dose, another person's perspective might help. We just can't keep going over the same ground."

"I'll do it," said Millie.

She smiled.

"But I'm not going to anyone you know through your work. I know, I know, I know. This isn't some competition between us to see who gets to choose the outcome. But I don't want you to have any home field advantage. I'm picking the person."

At this Edward laughed.

"I'll cede home field advantage to you, Mil. Pick whoever you want."

He reached across the counter and touched her shoulder. Again, they made eye contact.

"Chicken and carrots, okay?" she said.

"Sounds perfect," he said.

After dinner had been eaten, and after Edward had cleaned the dishes, they sat on the patio and looked at the stars. Edward shared anecdotes about his patients; Millie gave him the entire plot line of the book she was reading. They discussed family, and made tentative travel plans to both Indiana and northern New York for the upcoming holidays.

At ten, Edward announced that he was turning in. He kissed Millie on the way back into the house. Just a light brush across the corner of her mouth. That she slipped naked into bed with him a few minutes later surprised and pleased him. Hers was a terrific body that always aroused him. After years of being together, they knew each other's buttons to press. And they pressed them.

When they were finished and Edward lay back in the darkness, he couldn't help but wonder if his wife had remembered to take her pill.

When Mary Lou Litsky earned her master's degree in Psychology, she decided to use the significant inheritance she had recently received at the death of an uncle she did not know to open her own counseling center. She also decided to change her name to Meryl.

Meryl selected an old, two-story house a couple blocks from the downtown area of Roanoke. Her degree had been earned at nearby Weatherly College, and she hoped for a steady stream of referrals that would be sent her way from contacts at the school. She designed a sign with flowers overlaid on a night sky of stars, a comet and a smiling crescent moon. When it was finished and the sign company had hung it from the wooden frame they had dug into the front lawn, she took a picture of it and crafted an advertisement of sorts announcing the establishment of *The Garden of Healing*. She ran the ad in every newspaper and magazine she could find within a fifty mile radius. She also purchased air-time from a select number of radio stations to drum up business. Public Broadcast as well adult contemporary formats were good; rock and country were a waste of her money.

Meryl had been the oldest of her graduating class, deciding only after the age of forty that contributing to the general mental health and well-being of her community was what she really was meant to do. She had been a telemarketer, had sold ad space for a monthly newspaper and had waited tables. Her first marriage, to the owner of a store specializing in drug paraphernalia, ended within a year. Her second, to a man who wore his hair long, road a large and loud motorcycle, and made countless efforts to talk her into a threesome with the shapely young woman living in the house trailer next door, didn't make it six months.

She was just over five feet tall and wore loose-fitting, flowing dresses. Hers was not a delicate form, but she carried it comfortably. She lived alone in a one bedroom apartment near a shopping mall. She often proclaimed herself to be a vegetarian but enjoyed a chili-dog for lunch somewhat regularly. She wore contact lenses that made her blue eyes appear green; her black hair was almost always pulled back in a ponytail.

Millie Chase was not the first person to call her after seeing one of her ads, but she was among the first few of what had been a relatively short list.

"Yes, I do a fair amount of marriage counseling," said Meryl into the phone.

"Well, I believe I might like to set up an appointment for my husband and I to visit you," said Millie. "He works some crazy hours, so are you open at all over the weekend?"

The appointment was made for the following Saturday morning. Mille had second thoughts the moment she hung up the phone, but she was a woman of her word, and she had agreed to this. She also knew, from the hours of counseling they both had gone through after the death of their child, that something positive, something good, might come of this.

Edward and Mille stopped for coffee and croissants on the way into the larger city of Roanoke. They sat at a tiny table in an alcove at the front of the café, windows on three sides of them.

"Nervous?" he asked.

"No," she said. "It's an hour. It might do some good. If not, how bad could it be?"

"I asked around a bit about this place. It's apparently brand new. Not that that means anything one way or the other."

He parked the black BMW sedan on the street in front of *The Garden of Healing*.

"Catchy sign," he said as they walked to the front door.

Millie stopped at the porch.

"Listen," she said, "you have to go into this with an open mind. I promised you that I would, so you need to as well. No condescending *I'm a psychiatrist* crap, OK, Edward?"

"You're a hundred percent right, Mil. This was my idea, and I'm going to honor that."

The living room had been repurposed to accommodate counseling sessions. A sofa and a pair of matching easy-chairs were placed around a coffee table. A variety of crystals of different sizes and colors rested on the table. A sandbox sat in the corner of the room furthest from the windows. Candles were placed throughout the room. Each of them had been lighted.

"What brings you to me today?" asked Meryl after introductions had been made and seats taken.

Edward and Millie sat on the sofa; Meryl curled up, one foot tucked under her, in an easy chair.

"Do you want to go first?" said Edward.

Millie shook her head.

"We lost a baby," said Edward. "I don't really see the point in creeping up on this. We lost a baby five years ago, and we've not been able to fully cope with it since. It will not, and it should not ever go away. We both understand this. It's part of the healing process. But it continues to impact our marriage in a kind of unhealthy…"

"Edward wants me to have another baby," said Millie. "He hasn't stopped asking in five years. We fight about it all the time. I'm not willing to go through that again, and he just doesn't get it."

"It's not just that," said Edward. He was directing his remarks to Meryl. She sat without moving, her mouth slightly open.

"I hate it that Millie hasn't been able to move on just a bit more. I hate that for her. I understand depression, better than most people I understand it, but this is the first time in the last couple of years that Millie has agreed to discuss it with someone other than me."

He looked at his wife.

"I'm proud of you," he said.

"And stop treating me like I'm one of your patients, okay, Edward?"

They sat in a triangle of uncomfortable silence. Meryl wanted to suggest that each of them hold a crystal before continuing, but prudently swallowed that idea.

"I worked off and on after the baby," said Millie, "but nothing really ever seemed to come close to filling the emptiness. I'm not sure Edward has been able to see that."

She now turned to him.

"We've said all of this to each other before. A thousand times. I know you were hurt… I know you were devastated by the baby dying. I saw that, and it broke my heart, Edward. And I know I'm not the woman you married. I'm not the woman you fell in love with."

"That's not accurate," he said. "You are very much the woman I fell in love with. I just want you to get to a better place, emotionally and psychologically. Wouldn't you want that for me? Sure, I have an ulterior motive maybe. If you get to that place, maybe you'll consider another child. That's selfish of me, I know. But who loses if you take steps…if we take steps to make you happier?"

Meryl truly wanted to interject something in the few seconds of silence that followed. The expectation of a slow warming toward mutual confidences that she had anticipated this session would be had most certainly been left at the doorway. The tidal wave of emotion and honesty had overwhelmed her. She took one of the crystals, a blue one, off of the table in front of her and held it in her lap.

"Let's start with some breathing exercises. I think that they can often contribute to our mental and emotional processes," she said.

It was quiet for the first half of the drive home. As they neared Botetourt, Edward began, seemingly without any trigger, to laugh. Millie wanted desperately to remain in the cocoon of thought she had settled into but could not. Edward's laugh was infectious; she couldn't stop herself. Within seconds, tears were streaming freely down each of their faces. Edward had to pull the car over for safety's sake.

"How are your mental and emotional processes doing?" asked Edward.

They were back in their kitchen. He was sitting at the counter as Millie made sandwiches for lunch. Although the day was slightly overcast, the cream colored walls of the room seemed brighter.

"Didn't you learn any of that during your residency, Edward?

"You know, it's crazy, but the catharsis actually was pretty effective. It's true that when we share thoughts with someone and there's a third party present, we feel our message is getting through more clearly."

"Your messages always get through clearly, Edward. I just don't always respond to them."

"I know," he said.

He sat on the stool opposite his wife who stood while she ate her sandwich. That she often ate while not seated used to bother him. But he grew to love all things about her, and this idiosyncrasy was part of her.

As she leaned over her plate her black hair fell in front of her face. She took small bites from her sandwich behind the curtain. Her mouth was delicate, and she chewed with tightly closed lips without looking up.

"You think we should go back to see Meryl again?" he asked.

She looked up with a quizzical expression, as if she were contemplating what to order in a restaurant.

"Maybe not you," she said, "but I think I might. I think I might spend too much time by myself. I mean, I have the food pantry stuff, but that's not really communicating with anyone to any great extent. Would you mind if I saw her some more?"

He had just taken the last bite, a rather large one, of his sandwich. He held up a finger as he chewed.

"I think it's a good idea," he said. "People like that, people like Meryl can almost never do any harm."

Millie smirked.

"God, you have no idea how lofty you can sometimes sound. It's cute most of the time, but only because I know you. I know that you're actually not that way."

"It's not intended," he said. Then with a smile, "well, rarely is it intended."

"I promise I'll keep you posted," she said. "There might be some therapy stuff she suggests that would work on your patients."

"Anything for good emotional and mental processing."

Millie took his empty plate and placed it with her own in the sink.

"I might go upstairs and take a nap," she said.

She kissed the back of his neck and placed her hands, only for an instant, on his shoulders. He felt her leave the room as she headed for the stairs, and he wanted to follow.

Nuncia

"I'll tell you about myself, but you won't believe me," she said.

Nuncia Claro was sitting in Dr. Chase's office. It was her first morning at the Botetourt State Hospital, and she was being interviewed by the Director, the top dog. He wore a shirt and tie under his starched white coat. Edward Chase felt it important to speak with each patient as soon as possible after admission. This was a Tuesday morning, and he had carved out an hour before his next meeting.

"Well, Nuncia, why don't you give me a try. I'm a pretty believing person."

She sat opposite his large desk. Her hospital scrubs seemed one size too large for her small frame. She pulled her feet up and hugged her knees to her chest as she began.

Her hair was dark, and her eyes seemed black. She had the broad forehead often associated with indigenous peoples around the world. Her skin was the color of soft caramel. She spoke with an accent; her demeanor was one of confidence. She looked younger than the age of thirty that was registered in the medical intake chart that Edward held in his lap, but not by a lot.

"I was born in Panama, in a small village," she began with a shrug. "We had very little. There was a well in the middle of the village. We all used to go to fetch water. We had electricity, but it would go out for days at a time.

We used to walk two miles each day to catch a bus that would take us to school. My little sister and a cousin and me. We never left each other's side, even when we had to go in the bushes and pee. We were young, but there were bad boys who wouldn't have cared how young we were. We were taught by nuns.

When I was fifteen my mother died. I'm not sure what killed her. Maybe tuberculosis or something like that. She coughed and coughed.

So, I was left to raise my little sister. Even though she was only one year younger than me, it fell on my shoulders.

One day at school I was reading a newspaper. We used to read newspapers from the city to practice our English. I saw an advertisement looking for a kitchen helper. It was in the city…that was many miles away and you could only go there by a bus ride. That night, I asked my father to buy me a bus ticket. I told him if I got a job in the city, that I would send all the money I made back for him and for my sister.

He bought me a ticket to the city and gave me a little money. I look back on that and realize that it was a one way ticket. The money he gave me was not enough to buy a way home.

Anyway, when I got to the city, I had never seen so many people. I was terrified, to be honest. But what could I do? I asked a woman on the street for directions to the place that was looking for a kitchen worker. The address was in the advertisement I carried with me. It was a long way away, so she gave me a ride in her car. I will always pray for that woman. Her kindness.

The house was so huge. And I remember the doorbell sounding like the bells at a church," she said

Doctor Chase rose and went to a coffee pot placed on a small table adjacent to his desk.

"Would you like some coffee, Nuncia?"

"No. The coffee here is tasteless," she said. "I had some with breakfast."

He poured a cup and returned to his chair.

"Please," he said.

"So, this was the home of the Ambassador to Panama. The American Ambassador to Panama. Had I known that I never would have made such a foolish trip away from my village.

The woman who took me into the house, she was American and was dressed like in a magazine. We sat in the kitchen, and she gave me a glass of juice. The kitchen was almost larger than my whole house back home. The juice was delicious. I remember it was so cold and I was very thirsty.

She asked me if I could cook, and I told her that I could cook like I did for my father and little sister back in my village.

She asked me if I could clean, and I laughed. I told her that I had been cleaning up after people since before I could walk. All I could think of was that I was so happy that the nuns had worked so hard teaching us English.

And I think because she felt sorry for me that she gave me the job. And it was that easy to be out of my village. I lived in a tiny attic room in the big house now. I had to wear the same clothes as the other women and girls working at the house. Black dresses and shoes. Mostly, I cleaned and served meals. Standing perfectly straight in a line with the other workers behind the bigshots sitting at the dining room table.

But I also learned to cook. The head cook, the chef, his name was Robert and he had been trained at a culinary school in New York. He wasn't a whole lot older than me, and he liked me. Not in a boyfriend girlfriend kind of way, but something like that. He wanted to speak Spanish better, and I helped him with that.

And for the next two years, he taught me so much. Sauces, spices; real fine dining stuff."

"Were you able to go back to your village and see your family at all?" asked Edward.

"I sent them a letter, of course. As soon as it was determined that I was going to be living in the big house. And over the next couple years I took the bus to see them a few times. And I did what I promised I would do. I sent them money."

"That's a remarkable story, Nuncia. How impressive to think that a teenage girl could possess that much courage and fortitude to make her way into a position like that."

"Then they retired," she continued as if the doctor had not spoken. "They retired and moved to Florida. The mister, the ambassador, he told me that they didn't need any cooking or cleaning help in the new house they were moving to. He said it was a small house. But he did tell me that if I wanted to go to America, that he could get me the papers I needed to do that.

So, I made one last trip to my village to tell my father and sister that I was going to America. My sister cried and I told her that I would send for her to join me when I was able to.

My father, I think he just wanted to make sure I was going to continue to send him money.

And so, I went to America. I flew to Miami, Florida. I lied to the ambassador and the misses and told them I had an aunt in Miami. Which was not really a lie because a girl I grew up with actually had an aunt there. I just borrowed her."

"There you were at the airport in Miami with no contacts at all? Did you have any money? Did you have any idea where you'd go? What you'd do?"

"I had four hundred dollars."

Edward smiled and shook his head.

"You were right. I'm tempted not to believe you. But the story of your early life is too incredible not to be true. What did you do in Miami?"

"I went to a line of taxi cabs and told my driver…he spoke Spanish, but only like a Cuban…to take me to where the rich people live. So, he drove me to this area pretty far from the airport where there were huge houses. Almost as big as the embassy house in Panama City. He asked me what I was going to do, and I told him I was going to get a job. He turned out to be a nice man. He didn't even make me pay for the ride.

The first four houses I knocked on the door, they told me they didn't need any help. The fifth house was my lucky charm. The man who answered the door was the biggest person I've ever seen in my life. He was seven feet tall; a very slender black man.

When I told him I had just arrived to America from Panama and that I needed a job, he began to laugh. When he asked me if I was legal, I didn't know whether he meant my age or my papers to be in America, so I said yes.

When he asked me if I had any place to stay, I told him that I had stayed in the embassy house in Panama City where I worked. I told him that if I could stay in the house I cleaned and cooked in, that I would pay for it. I gave him my references, a letter from the ambassador and his wife, and he called them from another room as I sat in his kitchen. While he was on the phone, I snooped. The place was empty. No food, no fruit, no bread. The refrigerator only had bottles of beer and a package of cheese.

After he got off the phone, he told me that he'd pay me five hundred dollars a week, and that I could stay in one of the bedrooms. He told me that he traveled a lot, and that my job was to take care of the house, and to cook for him when he was there. Once again, fortune favored me."

Edward stood and walked to the coffee pot.

"Last chance," he said as he raised the pot in a gesture of offering.

Nuncia made a face as if she had just smelled sour milk.

"Please, Nuncia, go on," he said as he returned to his chair.

"He was a basketball player, a professional basketball player. He went to college in California, and he played for the Miami Heat. You know the Miami Heat?"

"Sure, I do. I played basketball in college. Not at that level, believe me."

"You're right," she said, "he would step on you like an insect."

"Don't hold your opinions back, Nuncia," he said, "I can take it."

At this she smiled. He took note of good teeth, of her strong jaw line.

"I worked for him, for Jawan, for six years. He moved to a new house in Fairfax, Virginia when the Miami team traded him, and he asked me to move with him."

"All this time," asked Edward, "were either of you in any sort of relationship? Did he have a girlfriend? Did you have a boyfriend?"

"I'll tell you the truth. Sometimes when he was traveling for basketball games, I did see a boy in Miami. He was a groundskeeper at a house nearby. I saw him out there working, and I went out to get the mail. Just so he'd see me. We were cozy together.

I think it was different for Jawan. The only people who came to the house were other men. I can't be sure, but I think Jawan liked boys. I think that's maybe the reason he wanted a young woman living in his house with him. To put on a show for everyone to see that he had a woman living there.

After he stopped playing basketball, he told me he was going to move back to California. He never really offered me a job to go with him, so I kind of took the hint. But it was okay. I had a lot of money in the bank...I saved every penny that I didn't send to my father. Jawan was very kind to me. He bought me everything and he gave me huge amounts of money for my birthday and Christmas."

"And that's when you started the restaurant?" asked Edward.

"No. not for a few years. I got an apartment in Fairfax. It was a dump compared to the houses I'd lived in. But it was mine. For the first time in my life, I had a place of my own.

I worked as an assistant chef at a very nice restaurant there in Fairfax. The training that guy Robert gave me back in Panama really came in handy. After a few years, I thought, why not? I can do this.

So, I called Jawan and asked him if he would be interested in an investment. I told him about my plan. I had a place picked out, and many of my co-workers were excited about working for me at my place.

Jawan told me that he'd have his business manager call me. I never even knew he had a business manager. But he called, this business manager. I sent him the budget I worked up, and the plans for inventory and staffing. Insurance and earnings and all of that. He told me later that he would advise Jawan to invest, but that it would mean a pretty high percentage of ownership for him. I didn't care. I was so excited I could have peed myself. Here I was, a little girl from Panama who had been in America less than ten years, and I was about to own my own restaurant."

"Where you nervous? Did you worry about failing?"

"No. Not one little bit. I never failed at anything. I never failed when I went to the embassy house in Panama. I never failed when I knocked on the door at Jawan's house in Miami. People who didn't work hard were the ones who failed. It wasn't my cards."

Here she was silent. She shrugged and stretched her legs out in front of her. She sat properly now; legs crossed with her hands resting on a knee.

"But it failed," he said.

Nuncia nodded.

"Yep, it failed. Eighty percent of all new restaurants fail within the first year. We made it six months. People just stopped coming. It's a tricky business, doctor. I felt bad for wasting Jawan's money, and that I couldn't send money home for quite a while. He was nice about it. I called him myself. I didn't want to hide behind his business manager. He told me if I needed anything, to let him know. He laughed when I asked him if he wanted to invest in another restaurant, and that made me feel a little better.

And now, here I am," she said as she recrossed her legs.

"Here you are," he said, "and I'm glad you're here."

"We'll see," she said with a shrug.

"May I ask you something, Nuncia?"

"You're the doctor," she said.

"Is the failure of your restaurant, is the fact that you lost a significant amount of Jawan's money…are those the reasons you wanted to hurt yourself?"

She had been looking at the floor in front of her feet. At his question, she looked up and directly into his eyes.

"No. It wasn't that. I'll tell you what makes me…what made me want to hurt myself. But not right now. I don't want to talk about it anymore."

Millie met him at the door. She was dressed as she usually dressed, in jeans and a tee shirt. Her feet were bare as they almost always seemed to be.

"Get changed and I'll get us a beer. I want to tell you about my session with Meryl."

She was waiting for him in the living room when he came down the stairs. She was crossed-legged in the easy chair she often sat in to read. More often than not, particularly in the last several weeks, this is where Edward found her when he came in from work.

She had placed an opened bottle of beer on the coffee table in front of the chair left vacant for him.

"Thanks," he said. "Cheers. So, tell me about Meryl."

"She was all clawed up. Her arms and hands were scratched all to shit. Apparently, she got a new cat, and the thing is half feral, or something."

"It's not going to be the only cat that woman ends up owning. I'm pretty confident in that prediction."

"It was not horrible, you know. We did our breathing exercises. We listened to a recording of waves rolling onto a beach. We held crystals in our laps for most of the time. But we also had some good conversation. She's kooky as all get out, don't get me wrong. But she's a very nice woman. When she asks you how you're feeling, you can tell she really wants to know."

"Patients will certainly see right through you if you if you let them off the hook by not pushing them to answer a question," he said.

Millie was silent for a moment. She had hoped that Edward's reaction to her recounting the meeting with Meryl would not be in the form of a critique. Edward was supremely intelligent and had twelve years of school, and two years of clinical practice under his belt. But he was also the son of a grocery store manager and part time secretary. He rarely afforded himself the opportunity to appear above it all.

He shook his head.

"I'm sorry, Mil. Occupational hazard. Butting in when it concerns anything related to treatment. I'll shut up and listen. What were the conversations about?"

"Thank you, Edward. I was surprised. She didn't want to talk a lot about the past. It was like she didn't want to drag me over those coals again. She asked a lot of questions about the present and the future. What I did now. Was I content with myself; with the person I am now? What did I see myself doing tomorrow, next week, next month and so on? I mean, it's not like we all don't think about those things, right? It just seemed a little more exposed…in a good way…to tell someone else about plans. About aspirations."

She sipped her beer. He sat and nodded.

"I decided to go back a few more times. To be honest, I was always a little bit indifferent towards the counseling we went through. And she's not the end-all be-all counselor, I get that. I actually feel more like I'm the one driving the bus with her, and that feels comfortable. I don't know if I'll get anything sorted out any better than I already have, but like you said, what can it hurt?"

"You clearly seem to be feeling like your old self a bit more. That's not a psychiatrist talking; that's your husband happily pointing out the obvious."

"I do feel like I've come out of the fog a little. I'm still not crazy about living here. We could have stayed in Rochester. But I'm going to try really hard not to dwell on that. There's something to Meryl insisting that we talk about the here and now, and about the future. I'm going to focus on that."

Edward was tempted to point out what he was thinking: that ignoring the past, particularly events from the past that could be identified as the genesis of problems experienced in the present, would never lead to lasting resolution. But his wife was smiling as she told him about the cat lady and sipped her beer. And this woman with her black hair and fiery smile was not his patient.

"I think that's all excellent news, Mil," he said.

"I wonder if it could be that simple?" she said. "I wonder if by just sitting down with some stranger-lady with cat scratches all over her arms and talking for an hour could have that kind of impact on someone? In the way they're feeling about stuff?"

"Sure, it could. Sometimes, just taking a first step can have a huge impact. Or it might just be the crystals," he said.

She smiled at this.

"Take me out to dinner, Edward. I want some Italian and I don't feel like cooking."

"This woman's life story is like nothing I've ever heard in my entire career. I kept wanting to accuse her of lying. Or embellishing, at the very least."

"Why is she there?"

They were enjoying a quiet meal at Sangiovese, a small Italian restaurant half-way back to Roanoke. Of the ten tables in the dining area, only three were occupied. Millie and Edward sat in the window and watched cars drive by. They shared a carafe of red wine that seemed, even to their unsophisticated palates, to have been poured out of a box. But the pasta was cooked perfectly, and the chicken was not dry.

"Suicide," he said. "Suicide attempt."

"That's awful. What was so interesting about her life story?"

Edward recounted in some detail the experiences of Nuncia's life.

"A basketball player? A guy in the NBA?"

"Yeah. She apparently just knocked on his door and became his house-keeper and he later invested in her restaurant. You can't make that up, can you?"

"Will she be alright? Do you think she'll try again?" Millie asked while chewing.

"The percentages say no," he said. "By far, people who survive a suicide attempt do not end up dying of suicide. A lot of that number is driven by the fact that many of the initial attempts aren't genuinely meant to cause death. You know? Calls for attention and that."

"Was that her case, do you think?"

He drank the last of his wine and wiped his mouth with the linen napkin.

"Way too early to tell. I can say this: she's an extremely complex woman. I don't think I've ever encountered anyone quite like her. I mean, you think about it, and here's this woman who comes literally out of the jungle and achieves a level of accomplishment and sophistication that's mind-boggling. She's complex, but she's also child-like."

"Take me home, Edward. I've had just the right amount to drink."

Father Dud

"I was a priest."

John Dudley and Edward Chase sat opposite each other in an alcove off the main lounge area of the hospital. Other patients currently residing at the facility were busy with group counseling or other activities. The two men, one very fit and handsome and wearing a white coat; the other, quite noticeably overweight and wearing the slate gray hospital scrubs that seemed omnipresent, had the room to themselves.

"Before we get going, John, I hope it's acceptable to you that we have this first discussion here in the lounge. My office is being painted, and the fumes would be a bit much even if we kicked the painters out for an hour."

"This is fine."

"I find that very interesting, that you were a priest. Before we talk about why you left the church, can you talk a little about what got you into it?"

Edward thought of Meryl's preference to ignore the past. His expression was unchanged.

"First off, I didn't leave the church. I haven't left the church. I left the priesthood."

Edward nodded.

"Good distinction. So, what appealed to you about going into the priesthood? Tell me what was the motivation to go that route in life? I'm guessing that in most cases that decision is made at a relatively early age. What took you down that path, John?"

John Dudley sat with his legs uncrossed and his hands on his knees; a basketball player sitting on the bench waiting for his turn to enter the game. The bandages on his wrists were in plain sight; he did not make any effort at all to hide them.

He was a large man, nearly as tall as Edward, but one would guess, close to a hundred pounds heavier. His face seemed swollen, but the fleshiness in his cheeks and neck was simply his normal look. He had extremely light blue eyes and the complexion of a hemophiliac. He had no facial hair but had done a poor job of shaving the last time he had razor in hand. He'd used an electric for the first time in his life, and several spots on his neck had been missed. He looked and acted far older than his forty-three years, and this bothered him not at all.

He inhaled deeply and exhaled with his mouth closed. The sound could have been an ancient animal, some fifty year-old bull enjoying a cleansing breath before lying down to die.

"I didn't pick the priesthood as much as it picked me, really," he said. "When I was a boy...I was one of those boys who didn't have a lot of friends. I had a couple, but not too many. I was what you'd call a loner. I stayed at home mostly. And I wasn't what you'd call studious or anything."

"Activities?"

"Not really. I liked comic books when I was a little kid. I read some a bit when I got older. The Hobbit. That kind of stuff. I watched a lot of television, I know that. Probably way too much."

Edward smiled and looked directly at the man seated across from him. John was reluctant to make eye contact.

"Back to why I became a priest. I think it just sort of presented itself as the only option. I was religious and all of that, but it wasn't like I burned with a fire to serve the Lord or anything. I just didn't really have any other plan. One of the young priests who was visiting our parish talked to me about it and the next thing you know, I'm going to seminary."

"What was that like, John? What was seminary like?"

"Like life."

John Dudley scratched the top of his head. His light brown hair stood up and pointed in all directions like a missing row of hay in a field a farmer has cut haphazardly. Again, he sighed.

"Explain that if you would, John."

"Did you play sports in school?" asked John. "I guess, because you're pretty tall, that you were a basketball player. Or maybe a football player. Or both. And you're a handsome guy; probably had lots of girlfriends. The whole package, right?"

"Not to the extent you might imagine, John. But let's get back to the seminary for a second. Was your family happy that you chose that as a career path?"

"My father died when I was seven. I really have very few memories of him. My mother was ecstatic. I remember the day she drove me there and dropped me off. She cried right before she left, but she told me they were tears of joy."

"That must be a nice image in your memory."

"The reason I asked that stuff about you, Doctor Chase, is that the life you had isn't even close to the life I had. I wasn't so much bullied as I was ignored. The other boys all through school, even in seminary, never made much of an effort to engage with me. I understand that. I was never one of the popular kids. Even as I was going through theology classes, learning Latin, all the stuff you do to become a priest, I kind of did all that in my own little circle, you know?"

"When you look back on that, John, when you revisit those times and experiences, how do you feel about that?"

John Dudley took another cleansing breath. His lips were closed and ever-so-slightly turned up for an instant at the corners.

"You're very good at what you do, Dr. Chase. I've taken a ton of psychology classes. One thing the Catholic Church does pretty well to prepare you for becoming a priest is that they make sure you have a certain comfort level in discussing uncomfortable issues with people. They know these discussions are coming and they want you ready to be able to handle them. You're really good."

Edward Chase smiled with genuine warmth.

"Thank you, John. And you're very observant."

"Well, I want to say it made me stronger," said John Dudley, "but I think a more accurate description is that it simply made me more apathetic. Some of the other men at seminary gave me the nickname of Father Dud. It was meant to be endearing, they said. Yeah, sure it was. But in reality, it didn't really phase me one way or the other. I just kind of got numb to a lot of things through the years. I know you understand that, even if that concept could never have happened to someone like you."

"I do understand it, and I'm going to guess that, in addition to this being some sort of defense mechanism that you employed, there was also a reluctance on your part to allow yourself to feel hurt or slighted. Why do you think you might have not allowed yourself to feel hurt or, at the very least, unsettled by the way the other boys and men treated you?"

"You a Catholic?

"I am not," said Edward. "I was raised as a Methodist."

"Catholics have forgotten more about guilt trips than all the other religions combined. We're absolute pros at guilt. It's the lifeblood of our whole existence. We're born guilty, for goodness' sake. Original sin and all that."

John Dudley's shoulders climbed and fell as he took in and released another large breath.

"Dr. Chase, I couldn't allow myself to feel hurt or bad about any of that because it would have been wallowing in my own weakness. In the eyes of the God I prayed to back then, it would have been a crutch. I needed to just take it and swallow it up. Absorb it and move on."

"You know any Catholics?"

"Not really the crowd I came up with," said Millie.

She and Edward were walking the cul-de-sac. His evening wardrobe had shifted from cargo shorts to a pair of jeans. The weather was cooling at night, and they both wore sweaters. Millie had not elected to add shoes to her outfit.

"Aren't your feet cold?"

"My feet are like dragon paws. Nothing can hurt me through my feet."

"Superpowers aside, be careful where you step."

"Why you want to know about Catholics?" she asked.

"New patient. A former priest. Appears to be wound incredibly tight."

"What's he in for?"

"Another suicide attempt," said Edward.

"Another one?" she asked. "Two in one week?"

"'Tis the season, I guess. Thanksgiving and Christmas on the horizon. There's data that supports that."

They passed the next two homes in silence. The foliage on the distant hillsides surrounding the neighborhood had begun to turn color. He took her hand.

"I miss the intensity of the leaves turning color in northern New York. The reds and yellows and oranges," he said. "Here, it just sort of goes from green to brown without a lot of variation."

"Nothing keeping us here except your job, Edward."

"I know, but that's a pretty big something."

Millie had wanted to stay in Rochester. Edward had been offered a job at the facility in which he had done his residency, but greater opportunities for growth and career development lay on the horizon. Specifically, the horizon of the Botetourt State Hospital situated in the foothills of the Blue Ridge Mountains. Many of the positions he had been offered paid more; one was even close to Indianapolis which, surprisingly, his wife had been against. But Botetourt had an opening for the Director of Mental Health, a position probably better-suited for someone with many more years of experience than he could claim. His competitive instinct kicked in. He liked the thought of being the Director of anything while still in his early thirties. And he knew deep down that his wife's reluctance to enthusiastically sign on for the move to Virginia was not so much about the location, but more about the emotional place she occupied internally. When she worked through that, through the long-lasting grief at the loss of their child, she would be happy living just about anywhere. Each of them took their love for granted, and they often expressed this. Their marriage was as strong as steel; neither of them ever considered living apart from one other. That thought would have been foreign and cold had either of them entertained it. And the bond between them would not lose one bit of strength, even as they moved away from their home in Rochester. They both knew this but expressed it differently.

As they neared their own lawn, he released her hand.

"I have to get something out of my car," he said.

"That was a shitty thing for me to say, Edward. I don't mean to bring up the same issue over and over. I'm always condemning you for doing that, and here I am doing it myself. Sorry."

He turned and walked back to her. He held her at the elbows and kissed her warmly, a sliver of tongue touching tongue.

"That was surprising, and very nice," she said.

"If we left, who would take care of my priest?" he said.

"And who would support my cat lady?" she answered.

Delilah Duncan

───────◇───────

She was sitting alone on one of the six folding chairs arranged in a circle when the other patients began to filter in for their group session. The tight and sexy body that had graced the cover of Rolling Stone Magazine and had adorned the bedroom walls of hundreds of thousands of teenage boys and girls had softened considerably; she now weighed almost three hundred pounds. Form-fitting black leather pants and tank tops were long ago given up for calf-length, roomy dresses. Her hospital scrubs were sized to fit a large man, and the pantlegs had been rolled up so as not to drag along the floor. The long black hair that used to hang over her face as she pouted her way through just one more break-up song was now cropped shorter than an inch.

Her canes, the type that grip the user's forearms and have hand holds extended from the shafts, were placed on the floor at the sides of her chair. Her eyes were abnormally large, as if the sockets were just barely able to hold them. Despite the weight she had gained since her glory years, her cheeks were sunken and concave. She sat with her ankles crossed. Her right arm rested on her thigh and moved in a seemingly involuntary motion forward and back; not a tremor so much as what might be seen as an attempt to scratch her leg. Over and over and over again. It did not stop.

"Oh my God. You're Delilah Duncan," said Tara, the youngest of the patients now taking their seats as they waited for Doctor Chase to join them. "I've listened to all of your songs. My parents had all of your albums."

Delilah smiled.

"Thank you for recognizing me," she said. "I've cut my hair as you can see."

"When you cut your hair, did you lose your superpower?" asked John Dudley.

"Huh?" from Delilah.

"You know. Samson and Delilah. From the bible. He loses his powers when his hair is cut off."

"That kind of rings a bell," said Delilah. "I guess."

John Dudley knew better than to speak up, and he most certainly knew better than to attempt to amuse anyone. Reminded of this shortcoming by Delilah's muted response, he sat silently and looked out one of the windows. It might be days before he felt like talking again.

"Good morning, everyone," said Edward as he strode into the room, shutting the door behind him.

"I see we've started to meet the new member of our group. In the event you don't know her, this is Delilah Duncan. She's going to be joining us here for a while. Welcome, Delilah."

Once the group was seated, Edward asked that each member recite their name.

"If you would like to, it's perfectly fine to mention why you're here. For everyone except Delilah, this will be past history, but there's nothing wrong with that."

"I'm Tara, and I'm an addict. Heroin. This is my second time in here, and hopefully my last."

"I'm John Dudley," he said as he held up his arms and bandaged wrists, visual aids to explain his presence.

"I'm Peter. I really don't know why I'm in here except that I was court-ordered by some judge. I think this is a bunch of bullshit."

The brief silence that followed this moment of awkwardness was broken by Edward.

"Nuncia?" he asked as he nodded toward her.

"I'm Nuncia," she said. She sat with her heels at the edge of the folding chair and hugged her knees.

"Okay. Well good morning again to everyone. This is our morning group session. I'd like to begin today by asking our newest member to share a little about herself with the rest of us. Before we do that, however, I want to mention to everyone that we need to treat Delilah the same as we treat everyone else. Yes, we've all heard of her. Many of us have listened to her songs. She's famous. But she's a person with strengths and weaknesses just like the rest of us. So, we need to be cognizant of that."

Then, with a hand gesture to his newest patient: "Delilah?"

"You'd think with all the times I've been interviewed and all the times I've been on stage that talking in front of people would be easy. And it used to be, before I got whatever it is I have. And there used to be drugs…that helped."

Edward and Tara smiled at this. The three others did not.

"Anyway, most of you probably know my story, at least a little of it. I had a pretty nice career for a pretty long time. That's unusual, especially in this business. But I got old, and I developed this involuntary tremor thing…MS kind of thing…and I got fat and couldn't perform anymore. And now I live in a big, beautiful house…not far from here, actually. And here I am."

Tara raised her hand. Delilah smiled at this, her hand continuing its forward backward movement.

"Can I ask why you're here? Dr. Chase, is it alright for me to ask this?"

"Sure, it is," he said. "But it's also alright if Delilah wishes to keep that private."

"I have self-destructive tendencies," said Delilah. "I drink way too much, and my manager thought it would do me good to spend some time here."

"There's nothing wrong with having a drink once in a while," said Peter.

"You're in here 'cause you want to be?" asked Nuncia holding the palms of her hands up in disbelief.

"Mental health leads to spiritual health which leads to physical health. All of mine are fucked up," said Delilah. "That's why I'm here."

"Sometimes, the dynamic of these groups kind of drives itself," said Edward.

He and Millie were sitting at the window table at Sangiovese. They had just been poured glasses of wine from their second carafe of Chianti.

"This isn't one of them. There's real tension. There are real walls of defense being built."

"What do you do in that case?" asked Millie.

"Follow protocol. Try to create an environment that allows them to trust the people around them. That's really the value of group sessions. It hopefully allows patients to develop mechanisms that will work when they go back out into the world. Anybody can develop trust in a one-on-one setting; in a group, though, that's where it can be really tough."

"Tell me more about the rock star," said Millie.

"Quite the life. She started going on tour when she was a young girl still…sixteen or so. Her mother traveled with her as protection and turned out to be just about the worst influence possible. Alcohol, drugs; she apparently screwed about everyone around. And in front of her daughter quite often. And so, here's Delilah following in her mother's footsteps. She didn't tell me any of this in group, by the way. This was in private. She told me that she had no idea how many men she's slept with. Certainly, in the several hundreds, she told me. I think that because she's been married a couple times, there are real trust and commitment issues going on there. It's obvious that she was deprived of so much in those formative years. She wasn't able to develop any kind of safety netting for the crap that came along later in life. She's sophisticated, traveled the world, all that. But almost childlike in her inability to take steps without direction from her business manager. That being said, she's unbelievably smart. I think she truly sees shortcomings in her emotional development and tries to deal with them.

"I had no idea she lives around here," said Millie.

The server delivered entrees: veal for Edward, mussels in white wine sauce for Millie.

"This manager, the guy who's been with her since she got famous, he comes from here. When she couldn't really go on tour and all that any longer, he bought her a house close to the farm where he grew up. I think he lives on the west coast now, but he's the father figure she never had."

Millie dipped an edge of bread in the wine sauce.

"This is really good," she said. "Want to try a mussel?"

He shook his head.

"I have some news," said Millie between bites of bread crust. "I'm giving some thought to going back to school. Finishing my degree," she said.

Edward looked up from his veal. He was smiling as he raised his glass in a toast.

"Spectacular news, Mil. Wonderful."

He was all questions and logistics for the remainder of their dinner and on the way home. She answered patiently and made no effort to hide her excitement. They made love that night, an occurrence that had become more spontaneous and that happened on a far more regular basis. When he lightly kissed her lips before leaving for the hospital the following morning, she smiled.

"I thought you were sleeping," he said.

"You woke me," she said. "You're prince fucking charming."

Gabi Dillon worked as a kitchen assistant in the hospital's cafeteria. She was energetic and diligent in the duties she had been assigned. She pre-made and packaged garden salads, she peeled potatoes, she chopped vegetables, she transferred cooked dishes from pots and pans to metal cafeteria serving reservoirs. She also washed the pots and pans at the end of each meal and made sure every one of the trays the patients used were run through a giant dishwashing machine.

She wore her brown hair to just below ear level but went through her day wearing a hair net. She was not tall, and she moved with a sprightly delicateness. She enjoyed reading and could be seen with a book when she took her own meal breaks. In nearly every instance of interaction with others she was the person who had initiated it.

She loved standing behind the long serving table and portioning out large spoonfuls of food to the patients as they side-stepped along, trays in hand. She greeted each one before serving them and she wished each person a good day as they slid past.

"I don't even know why you serve this."

This was from Nuncia. She had placed a salad on her tray and was now at the entrée section of the production line.

"What is this supposed to be? Some wort of lasagna?"

"Yes, it is," said Gabi. "I tried a little when Mrs. Pike started to let it set up. It's really good. You might like it."

"I might like it, but I'd have to taste it first. There's no flavor in anything you cook here. Just give me a roll and butter."

Gabi picked up a roll with metal tongs and placed it on Nuncia's tray.

"Butter's right there," she said pointing to a glass bowl filled with individual pads of butter resting in a bed of ice.

"And it would be nice to get real silverware," said Nuncia. "Do you think we're going to spoon ourselves to death? These plastics are useless."

"I'm sorry," said Gabi. "I just do what I'm told."

"Welcome to the restaurant business," said Nuncia and moved to the large, circular table.

Gabi's dark eyes welled with tears as John Dudley took his place in front of her.

"She's probably having a bad day," he said. "Please don't be offended or hurt by anything she just said. I think you're doing a great job here, and I think the food is very good."

"Thank you," she said. "Would you like some lasagna?"

"I love lasagna. I might be back for more," said John.

"I'll be here," said the young woman.

She had recovered from Nuncia's rudeness and was once again loving the air she breathed. Hers was a world of light, of kindness and of finding the best in people. She knew, deep down, that even Nuncia had to smile occasionally.

John Dudley walked to the round table as if joining compatriots at a wedding reception. He placed his tray and plastic cup of water in front of the chair next to Nuncia's.

"May I?" he asked.

She shrugged, indifferent to his request.

He sat down with an exhale.

Delilah Duncan caned herself with some difficulty and took the seat on Nuncia's open flank. The two seats remaining empty were for Tara and Peter who were apparently going to be late for lunch.

"I think they have to make the food to a certain blandness," said John. "I don't think they can spice it up but so much for dietary reasons."

"You're a priest, right? Isn't that what you said in group? That you used to be a priest?"

"Yes," he said.

"Then why don't you keep to priest stuff and leave the flavor of the world to me, okay."

Admonished, John Dudley re-entered the cave of his existence. He ate his lasagna silently, but with gusto.

Gabi delivered a tray of salad, lasagna and a roll to Delilah.

"Here you are," she said. "I hope you enjoy it."

"I'm sure I will, sweetheart. The Father sure seems to be."

That evening, after the patients had retired to their individual rooms for the last hour before lights were to go out, there was a gentle knock on John Dudley's door.

He was lying on his bed and reading a travel magazine. "Yes?"

The door opened slowly. Nuncia's head poked into the room.

"Father, I just want to say sorry for the crack about being a priest. I am having a shitty day. That's not an excuse; we're all having shitty days, or we wouldn't be here. Anyway... sorry."

"Thank you," he said. "See you in the morning at breakfast. Maybe the food will be better."

He smiled at his light-hearted comment. It was a perfect balance between cutting the tension and suggesting that she play better with Gabi and the cooking team in the morning. It was priestlike.

Nuncia shrugged and pulled her head back out of the room. The door closed with a click.

After he had turned off his bedside reading lamp, and after he had lay in quiet darkness and performed the same nightly prayers he had recited in his head since he was a young boy, John Dudley thought about Nuncia. She had goodness in her, of course. Father Dud knew that all of God's creatures were capable of kindness. But Nuncia's goodness was varnished over with a patina of anger. And it seemed completely out of character that she had made this late-night visit to apologize. That had surprised him.

What he did not know, what he could not have known, was that only moments before Nuncia had rapped on his door, she had been visited by Delilah Duncan. Delilah had caned down the hallway and asked to speak to her. The discussion was along the lines of karma.

"I don't know shit about anything," Delilah had told her. "But I know this: if we don't take responsibility for the way we impact other people around us, that's a slippery slope. I'm just saying."

In the seconds that intervened between this conversation and Nuncia's decision to visit the Father, the young woman from Panama thought of her mother. And she was unable to remember a time in her life following the death of her mother when anyone had provided guidance of any sort like that which she had just received from Delilah, except of course, in a kitchen.

From the Journal of Nuncia Claro

I don't like to write. I have never been a good writer, especially in English. But this is what Doctor Chase wants each of us to do.

I asked him if he would be reading our journals, and he said no, they were for our expression of thoughts and feelings, or something like that. I thought about writing in Spanish, but America is my home now and English is my language.

The food here is terrible. It is tasteless and not fresh. I offered to help, but Doctor Chase told me that there are very strict rules about who can help prepare the food. He is a nice man, but his butthole is very tight. Everything is by the books with him.

I had a little argument with the priest today after our group meeting in the morning. I made a tiny gripe about the food while I was in the serving line, and he scolded me in that sneaky priesty way that they do. Without really telling you that you've done a sin, they sneak the sin into your pocket for you to deal with. I'm not playing that game. I don't care if he's a priest. I don't care if God is angry with me. After what happened to Claudia, I don't think that there even is a God. Let alone one who cares a shit about me and Father Fatso.

When Delilah came into my room to talk to me about the whole conversation the priest and I had had, I felt a little ashamed. I took out my feelings on the little girl who served the food to us. She did nothing to deserve that, and Miss Delilah told me that. So, I went to visit the priest in his room, and I told him I was sorry. I wasn't really sorry, but it looks like all of us are going to be in here at least a month or more. And I don't want any enemies, not even a priest.

After we eat our lunch at the big round table, the priest clears everyone's trays and throws away the plastic silverware they give us to eat with. That part is funny. The plastic silverware. Like Father Fatso is going to try to cut his wrists open again with that little white knife. But it is a nice gesture for him to wait on all of us. Maybe he committed some sin and he's trying to get even with God.

In the group today the young guy Peter lost his temper. I think he's in here because he drinks too much and fights with people. My father drank whenever he could, but he is not an angry man. Peter is an angry boy. He hates it here. Let's face the music, we all hate it here. But this is where we have to be for a while, so we need to settle into our seats and deal with it.

Miss Delilah and I sat in the window and talked for a long time this afternoon. She asked me a lot about my history, and I told her about the good fortune I had been blessed with. She told me that if my story were not so far-fetched and crazy, that it would not be believable. Where have I heard that before?

Miss Delilah and I sat in our window again and talked for over an hour. They keep you busy in this place. They don't want to give you a lot of time to feel sorry for yourself or to think about harming yourself again. But the free time is ours to use as we please. And Delilah and I enjoy talking.

The girl, Tara, is too young for us. She has no life experiences and nothing to add. But Delilah and I have been around the blocks.

The priest, Father Fatso, keeps to himself. And Peter just counts the days until he can get out and get drunk and beat someone up again.

We had an outing today. They brought a bus to the main entrance, and we all piled in like school children. Right after lunch.

We went to a bowling alley. I've been living in America for ten years plus, and it was my first time in a bowling alley. Not one of us was any good at it. My bowling balls kept going in the troughs on each side. The gutters. It was pathetic. But it was fun.

Peter, that angry boy, tried to order a drink from the bar on his way to the bathroom, but one of the hospital men followed him and caught him in the act. Peter was angry, but the hospital worker is a big Black man. Like Jawan, but more muscles. Peter is a lot of air.

Father Fatso was the best. He offered me some tips on how to keep my balls out of the troughs. And sometimes they worked. Maybe he's not such a bad guy after all.

Delilah talked a lot today about being a music star. We sat in our window and looked at the mountains out in the distance. It snowed a little bit over night, and it looked like sprinkled sugar on the hills.

She told me that when she was very young, she played her guitar and sang songs in a coffee shop. This was in California. A man from a music company heard her, and the rest was history. When she began to travel, her mother went with her for protection against all the things that happen to young girls on their own. I know a little about that.

But her mother was the opposite. Her mother had sex with many men, sometimes even in front of Delilah. Then it was Delilah's turn, and her mother told her to have sex with people that would help her career. And she made her do this in front of her. Can you imagine?

When Delilah told me these things, she cried a little. I can't even think of going through those things. My own mother, even though she was dead, gave me and Claudia more protection than that. Even from the grave.

More about Delilah's bad mother. She took all of the money Delilah was making, and it was a lot of money. She told me that she has sold many millions of albums over her life. I don't know what her cut is, but that's a lot of dough ray me. In the end, when she was still very young, she got all the money back and cut her mother out of the deal. She's pretty rich. I keep finding myself rubbing elbows with rich people. First the Ambassador, then Jawan, now Miss Delilah. I think she's the richest out of all of them.

Jesus, Mary and Joseph. The kids got caught having sex this morning. We all knew that they were sneaking off and doing it behind closed doors. I think that even the staff people, Eric, that big Black guy and some of the others, I'm pretty sure they knew and turned the other cheek. What harm was it doing?

But they were in the girl's, in Tara's room, going at it and one of the nurses walked in on them. Probably not the first time that's happened. Anyway, they sent that boy Peter to a different place, or a different part of the hospital. We were all sitting in our group meeting and heard him screaming at them from down the hall. He was using some choice language, let me tell you. I asked Doctor Chase if he would be moved permanently, and he said he was not sure.

I don't know what the big deal is. I've had sex a few times, with a few different boys, and don't really see what the big fuss is about.

Delilah asked me today if I would mind if she invited the girl, Tara, to sit in the window with us while we chat. I said that it was fine with me. The more, the merrier. So, she put her crutches on and went to the other side of the big room and got her. I feel sorry for Delilah that she has this disease. She has to feel like she has to depend on people, and I think that bothers her. She seems to me to be a very proud and independent woman…just like me. But I have seen her fall asleep sometimes in the late afternoon, sitting in a big chair in the sunlight. And when she sleeps, her arm and hand stop moving. Almost like God, if there is a God, is giving her a little break from this disease that almost never seems to allow her to be calm.

I hope that Tara decides not to do heroin anymore once she gets out of this place. Drugs are horrible business. Ask anyone from my part of the world, and they'll all say the same thing. Except for the bad men who get rich from selling them. Tara comes from a good family. When they allow visiting on Sunday afternoons, her parents are there to sit and talk to her. They seem to be upper crusted people. They dress nice and are very groomed. Probably not as wealthy as Delilah or Jawan; comfortable, as they say.

She told Delilah and me that she got started doing heroin when she was fifteen, and that her father's business partner, some man in his forties, was the one who gave it to her. She was sneaking around with this old man, meeting him in hotel rooms, and he got her hooked. The disgusting part of what she told us was that this man never got in trouble. He never went to jail. He just had to get a new business partner.

Lucky Friday. At group today, Father Fatso asked Doctor Chase if anyone new was going to be joining our morning group sessions. It was possible, said Doctor Chase, but was depending on how many new patients they took in. Doctor Chase also told us that the angry boy Peter was doing well and might be coming back to us.

Delilah said that we almost had a second group session in the afternoons, just by ourselves. It was three out of the four of us that sat and discussed things. I think this made Father Fatso sad. I felt like he felt left out. So, I blurted out that he should sit with us in the window. He said that he would like to, and he smiled. But it was a very sad smile, believe me. I'm not sure why I asked him. I just did.

Go figure that today, the first day the Father joins us, we decide to talk about sex. Maybe the priest in him brought that out in us. Delilah told us that she had been pregnant twice and had gotten abortions both times. I looked at the Father to see his reaction. You know priests and abortion… they don't mix. He just looked the same. No emotion. Tara told us that her father's business partner gave her a venereal disease, but that she had gone to a doctor and had been fixed from it. I told them that I had a very small sexual background. I said that sex was okay, but I wasn't going to put my life on hold and wait around for it.

The Father seemed uneasy when we were talking about it. Finally, he told us that he had never had sex. I wanted to ask him if that included little boys. You know those priests and their little boys. But I didn't, thank God.

We talked about parents today. At the group session in the morning and also when we sat in the window. I talked about the death of my mother and how that turned me instantly into the woman of the house. The Father said that that was probably why I had been able to accomplish the things I had. That I was independent. He pointed out that, even from the grave, my mother was a factor in the woman I became. I liked this. I've always felt like my mother was watching over me and Claudia. This priest, he's not such a pain in the you-know-what after all.

I asked him about his parents, and it was the opposite. His father died when he was a boy, and it did the opposite. He became too dependent on his mother. This is what he told us. He was a mama's boy; this is the word he used. But he smiled when he said it. He told us how the other boys teased him because he was chubby and did not play sports. He told us how the girls at his school used to point at him and giggle. This made me sad. I need to start calling him something other than Father Fatso in my journal. And I need to find those girls from his school and cut their hair off. Shave their heads and then giggle at them.

Father Dud. This is what I'm going to call him instead of Father Fatso. That would be a sin if that ever slipped out of my mouth. He told us that at priest school, the other men called him Father Dud, and that it was a term of endearment. That's the words he used. Term of endearment. I think that probably the other priest men were making fun of him, but if he likes to be called that now, that's fine with me.

Tara asked him today why he tried to kill himself. Sometimes from the mouths of children. That's one thing none of us have asked the other about. Why?

He shifted a little in his chair. He was uncomfortable, but who wouldn't be? I know that better than almost anyone. I don't want to talk about my reasons.

He only said that there had been someone who he could have helped, but didn't know how to, and that that someone had done harm to himself. He said that if he'd been a stronger person, he might have been able to prevent it all from happening.

From the Journal of John Dudley

I am impressed with the way Doctor Chase conducts the group sessions. I've counselled lots of people over the years from trivial matters to, literally, life and death. But almost never in a group setting.

I actually like the idea of keeping a journal. I've done this since I was very young, and this will just be a continuation of that practice. I suspect that eventually I will write the narrative of what happened that caused me to want to harm myself. That's such a lame use of those words. I didn't want to harm myself; I wanted to end my existence as I know it now to be.

A couple of people in my group are interesting. There is a young woman from Central America who defied all odds and ended up living in America and owning a very up-scale restaurant. She seems to be completely self-contained and does not want to speak to anyone. I believe she was a suicide attempt, but don't know that for certain. She has lots of anger built up, and she seems apathetic as to whether or not she hurts those around her when it comes out.

There is also a former rock star. A real one. Delilah Duncan. Even I, a guy with no real appreciation of music of any kind, have heard of her. She's from California and toured the world in her heyday. She seems to be afflicted with something like MS. Involuntary tremors of her right hand and arm. She seems kind, but very, very sad.

We also have a couple of kids in the group. A young woman who is trying to beat an addiction to heroin. I've seen this with several parishioners' children over the years. It can be done, but I wonder does the craving ever totally go away. I suspect not.

The young man in our group is a bottle-rocket waiting to have its fuse lit. In my opinion, he drinks to excess in an effort to harm himself, and then he lashes out. He's here because the court ordered it. Apparently, there is a history of assault. And it all comes from his anger. Maybe, while he's here, someone can get to the core of that. He's not going to move past this behavior pattern if they don't.

And just when you think that you cannot be surprised anymore, you get surprised. This is what Father Marconi used to tell us all the time at seminary. Don't ever get complacent in your views of the world and those in it. Something will surprise you, even when you think it not possible.

The chef woman from Panama, Nuncia, barked at the young woman serving our lunch today. It was lasagna, by the way, and was very good. Granted, the level of sophistication in the cooking is not up to what Nuncia is used to. But it's a cafeteria, for God sakes. I said something positive to the woman, and then I mentioned to Nuncia that she had been a bit tough on the girl.

I am relatively sure that Nuncia was raised in the Catholic Church. Nothing in her behavior tells me that, but the odds are very good that anyone coming from that part of the world was. But whatever deference she once held for the priesthood is long gone. In a very clear voice, she told me to mind my own business. That didn't surprise me. That she visited my room later this evening to apologize, that was the surprise. She is a complicated woman carrying a whole lot of baggage around.

It'll be interesting to see how she behaves with the cafeteria girl at breakfast tomorrow.

We have settled into a routine, all of the patients and Doctor Chase and his staff. Certainly, by design, we are not given much down time. Idle hands, and all of that. And I wonder once again if my act of attempting to end myself (and I have a difficult time even writing the word suicide) is a sin in the eyes of God. Of course, Father Marconi would say yes. But his world within the priesthood was not as complicated as was mine. He was not, I'll bet, faced with moral dilemma the way we were. The way I was.

I am paying close attention to everything I am told. I have to believe that there is something on my horizon that is good, that allows me to do good for others.

And my wrists are healing under the bandages, but now they itch like the devil.

I began to catalogue the variety of reasons the different members of our group are here. Not the events so much as the motivations. The young man Peter continues to smolder. He lost his temper again today and had to be removed by one of the big attendants. I must honestly say that I have never interacted with anyone like him. In the priesthood, by the time they get to you to ask for guidance or help, they've pretty much conceded that there is, in fact, something wrong with their own coping mechanisms. They've accepted the fact that they are the issue at hand, that they are the problem. The priesthood can be the last chance many people have as a healing resource. How could anyone ever take advantage of that position and cause more harm to someone fragile and vulnerable? I've been asking myself that question for ages and can't seem to find an answer other than that evil exists in the world. Comforting.

Nuncia, the woman from Panama, mentioned a father and sister who remained behind when she left her hometown, her village, and started her crazy and improbable journey to America. She mentioned more than once that she had been a source of financial support for them, sending money back whenever she could. Nuncia owned a restaurant that apparently failed, so I'm guessing that she was unable to continue to do this. Guilt is a horrible and almost always wasted emotion. Ask any Catholic this, and you'll get the same response.

I suspect Tara has the best chance of all of us to walk out of this place whole. She talks a great deal about her parents and her grandparents. She clearly comes from an upscale environment, and that provides her with an enormous advantage. Among other things, her parents will be able to afford on-going counseling and treatment if she needs it. Again, how could a fellow traveler in life so carelessly impact this woman's future by introducing her to an addictive drug like heroin? Is that calculated cruelty, or simply an unwillingness to own consequences we call into creation?

I must admit to being a touch starstruck when it comes to Delilah. Starstruck and saddened. We have all seen the posters and album covers of her when she was young and perfect. Lord, what a singing voice, and so attractive. And to now be so overweight and living through the dilapidation of her body and the uselessness of her muscles must be very difficult. I wonder what she dreams about: the old Delilah, on stage and partying with her fellow rock stars after the performances, or the new Delilah, trapped in a body that seems to be betraying her? Maybe I'll ask her.

In our group session this morning, Tara spoke up about the steps necessary for recovery from addiction. She seems committed, and I certainly hope she is successful. She's very pretty. Petite, like the lunch girl Gabi, but softer features. I do not know the real color of her hair, but for now it appears to be somewhere between platinum blonde and jet black. Not blended, but separate colors in one head of hair.

She has the body of a dancer. She eats very little, and she shared with us that she has tattoos circling each of her nipples. I will take her word for that. I am surely tempted to give that image a place in my head but will not.

The first step, of course, is to let go and let God. I understand the concept, but never really agreed with that as a critical part of the process. Addiction is an entirely personal condition. Obviously, many people need assistance of some sort to conquer it, but all decisions they make, starting with the decision to seek help, are theirs alone. They make the decisions and then they own them. God can assist; He can ride along as a wingman. But the person suffering through the affliction really has to be the one to drive.

Which brings me to the question of my own faith. I have faith in the existence of evil in the world. Good exists also, but I have seen evil, and it is real. Faith in God? I'll leave that to another entry.

I spoke privately with Doctor Chase this afternoon. He asked how I thought I was doing. Interesting distinction. Not how I was doing, but how I thought I was doing. Implied in that question is the fact that my response might not be reality. This caused me to wonder if people in his profession, people who live most of their lives surrounded by addicts, suicides, poor mental health sufferers and the rest, if they struggle in the own personal lives to stay somewhat normal. I'm told that psychiatrists often have a therapist of their own on the side. This makes sense to me. This would work in the priesthood, but only if people were moral. The little boy that sent me here needed my help. If I had had someone moral with whom to share what I knew about this boy instead of a man completely motivated by opportunism, so many lives would have been altered in a positive way. And I wouldn't have these bandages on my wrists, and I wouldn't be itching like crazy.

I knew some sort of outing was coming. Bowling. It's standard fair in closed facilities like this. Get the patients out into the real world so that they can begin to process the fact that their healthier lifestyle and the decisions that are driving it are not necessarily tied to the environment they find themselves in. Even though the patients have no genuine control over what happens on the outing, they can start to claim a bit of ownership simply because there exists the appearance of being out on their own.

A couple of developments intrigued me. On the positive side, Nuncia allowed me to give her a few pointers on bowling. I suggested she try the two-handed method often used by small children; her rolls consistently found the gutters, and I thought this might help. But she refused to, in her words, look like a retard...poor choice of words, but honest. She knocked some pins down and this made her laugh. She has a very nice smile with very white, very perfect teeth. Despite the thorny exterior, she has quite a fetching quality to her. It was nice to see her smile.

The more negative incident involved Peter. Brazenly, he ordered a drink from the bar on his way to the bathroom. One of the orderlies caught him in the act. It probably did not need to escalate into the scene it did, the big orderly and one of Doctor Chase's staff backing him into a corner, not just metaphorically. A bit of calm could have gone a long way.

Peter refused to participate and sat in silence as the rest of us finished our games. I sat beside him on the bus ride back to the hospital. I didn't speak to him on purpose. His anger drives his actions...all of them. If he ever decides to look for the root cause, particularly if he ever decides to seek help in doing so, there must be a solid sense of trust with whoever he opens up to. Diving right into that would only push him further into his unhealthy space. I would like to talk with him but know better than to initiate that. So, I sat beside him and was quiet.

In the afternoons, Delilah and Nuncia sit alone in an alcove in the main room. They have quite taken to each other. It doesn't take a rocket scientist to figure out the dynamic. Nuncia's mother apparently died when she was a little girl.

And, to the best of my knowledge, Delilah never had any children. Hence the surrogate mother-daughter relationship. It's clearly a positive development, but I worry about what will happen when or if we all get out of here. That's a lot of responsibility each of those women is taking on.

Lunch today was build-your-own tacos, and they were very good. Nuncia mentioned to Gabi, the young woman who serves us our food, that a little cilantro would really add to the flavor profile...her words, not mine. Gabi said that she would mention this to the head cook. A few days ago, I am certain that Nuncia would have fired something back along the lines of the cook not knowing a thing about flavor profiles. But today, she simply made that shrug of the shoulders and turned-up nose-face that we all are beginning to recognize. Self-progress, I guess.

I wonder what sort of life each of the people who work here go home to. I see Doctor Chase as an unpretentious man. He wears a wedding ring, and I'm guessing that his wife is very attractive and no doubt intelligent. There is a picture of the two of them on the credenza behind his desk, but the image is a bit far away from my seat on the opposite side of his desk to see clearly. The next time I'm soloing with him, I may ask if he minds if I take a closer look.

Gabi, our server girl, is nothing short of adorable. I asked her at lunch the other day if she lived close to the hospital. She told me that her trailer was a twenty minute bus ride away, but that she enjoyed the trips each day. She also mentioned that her girlfriend drove her occasionally, but not very often. Many people would wonder if the term of girlfriend was used romantically or platonically, but I truly don't care. As I wrote a second ago, she's adorable. Her brown eyes seem always to be seeking an excuse to light up with a smile.

Eric, the large man who attends to everything, goes to the weight room. I've learned that he played football in college, and that he's taking night classes toward a degree in some sort of social science. He's the strong and silent type, and I've only ever seen him in conversation with Gabi or the head cook.

As a surprise to absolutely no one, Peter was caught in Tara's room this morning right before group. Romantic relationships with people in recovery are terrifically dangerous. One might think that the support and closeness would be healing agents, and they certainly can be. But the potential downside of one of these relationships ending badly is terrifying. People in recovery are fragile enough as it is. Throw in a high dose of depression and possible anger, and you've got yourself a very dangerous situation.

They are both very attractive young people. In a different situation, I would probably see them and smile. They make a cute couple, as they say.

Sex is a tricky subject for me, and not simply because I took vows never to dabble with it. I always questioned the validity of a celibate man offering guidance on the subject of sex. My own experience is limited to the time when I was seven or eight years old and was tied to a tree by a couple of older girls. They pulled my pants down for a few seconds before releasing me. And this is the foundation of experience from which I am supposed to offer up insightful advice? Before deciding to go into the priesthood, I worried about the secular, person-to-person interactions that I would inevitably be involved in. Trust me, sex is just one of those elements many of us had no personal experience to call upon.

Peter was whisked off to another part of the hospital. His language as they took him away was creative. Poor Tara sat through our group session on her folding chair and stared at the floor. Intense fragility personified.

At our group session this morning, I shared my dream from last night of the only fight I've ever been in, clearly some sort of subconscious response to Peter being forcefully taken to another part of the hospital yesterday. I believe it was when we were all in the fourth grade when Debbie somebody-or-other decided to beat up all the boys in our class. I told the group that fights at that age consisted of grabbing someone and pushing them to the ground. Very little punching or kicking, thank God. Because I was very clearly the easiest target, she picked me to beat up first. I was terrified, of course, and most certainly had no idea how to fight, let alone against a girl. One advantage I had was that I was as big as Debbie; most of the other boys had not had a growth spurt, and they were both shorter and less filled out. She slapped me hard across the face two or three times and then pushed me to the ground. I went down pretty easily and covered my face with both hands and started to cry.

Nuncia asked me if any of the boys were able to beat Debbie. I told her that I didn't recall anyone claiming to have beaten her, but that I didn't go watch the fights the way the other boys did. She gave me her patented shrug. I think she approved. She told us that she beat up a boy when she was about ten and still living in her village. He had wanted her and her sister to remove their shorts to give him a peek (her words). She told us she hit him like a boxer would and then kicked him like a soccer player when he was lying on the ground. This made the group laugh, and laughter is a rare commodity in this environment.

Tara has begun to sit with Nuncia and Delilah in the afternoons. She's quiet, especially after having been caught alone in her room with Peter. I'm glad that the other women invited her to chat with them. I'm pretty sure from looking over Tara's parents on visiting days that she's had a good upbringing. I'd bet money on it that her mother has been a strong role model. But she's alone in here, as we all are alone in here, and by inviting her to join them, Delilah and Nuncia have done a very good thing.

Tara is very solicitous towards Delilah. She fetches her paper cups of juice and gently places a blanket over her lap when the sun is not shining. They have given Tara a drug... probably methadone...to curb her cravings. I know from a parishioner's experience with a son who was addicted that this treatment can be very effective. If I pray again, I will pray that this works for Tara. She strikes such a sorrowful pose with her rail-thin frame and sunken cheeks. You can barely detect her body under the hospital scrubs she wears. Almost as if she's not in there at all.

Nuncia surprised me today by inviting me to sit with them in their afternoon chat sessions. She was telling Doctor Chase that these pow-wows were as interesting as our formal sessions. I suspect she may have felt sorry for me that I was the only one left out. Whatever the motive, I am pleased to be among them now. I don't know what I'll be able to add, but it beats hell out of sitting by myself with a book.

Right out of the gate, the discussion turned to sexual experiences. It started with Tara asking the group where we all thought Peter had been taken to. I attempted to explain the dangers in getting involved during recovery or rehab, but this fell on deaf ears for the most part.

Delilah's sexual experiences were by far the most diverse and prolific. I remain stunned that people, especially women, can talk so openly about sexual experiences in front of me. It may have something to do with the fact that I was a priest, kind of a confessional thing. But for whatever reason, they simply open up.

I remember the first time I heard a confession, and I wasn't even ordained at the time, some friend of my great aunt was desperate to confess her sins, and she asked if I could hear her confession. My mother and I were visiting my great aunt and agreed to help this group of older women clean up this abandoned church. Out of nowhere, one of my aunt's friends asked me to hear her confession. I was still in seminary. I had no right to hear anyone's confession. It was probably a sin that I even went through with it. But something in me told me that it was of great importance to this woman, so I agreed. She was older. I remember her as being very tall, as tall as I am, and thin. Her fingers looked like she had spent her entire life knitting.

Even *she* talked to me quite openly about sex…well, sex with herself in the bathtub as I recall. The point is that some of us simply invite these discussions without actually inviting them. It's a confidence level a lot of these people have that they can talk frankly with us. A gift in a way. And a curse.

After hearing about many sexual encounters and not infrequent abortions and sexually transmitted diseases, mostly from Delilah, the conversation came around to me. I was dreading this, but I didn't want to appear as if I was not a team-player. I told the group that I had never had sexual relations with anyone. A vow of celibacy and all of that. This was met with silence which made me even more uncomfortable. Finally, Nuncia broke the silence. Who else but Nuncia? She told me that I needed to get laid. Maybe that way, she said, you won't want to slice your wrists open again.

Nuncia has begun calling me Father Dud after I told her the other men at seminary called me that. I still think there was an element of ridicule in the nickname they gave me, but I somewhat enjoy the way Nuncia says it. It's a bond in a way.

The old doubt will not go entirely away. Before I took my vows, I almost quit seminary. Not because of any lack of calling to do the Lord's will, but because I was unsure if I was the right kind of man to do it. I felt a strong desire to help people in His name, but I wondered if I had the skill set to accomplish much of this. I feel the same way today, even more so after failing so miserably at the biggest opportunity I was handed.

I picture myself in a variety of scenarios, and it's a stretch to think that I could be successful, even to some slight degree. What if I answered phones at a suicide hotline? What if I failed to express myself clearly enough? What if I didn't react properly to something I was told? I've never been anything close to forceful in my opinions or in my demeanor. I have lacked that since childhood. I was babied by my mother, and never developed much of a backbone, I'm afraid. What good am I ever going to be able to do for someone in need of firm guidance and support?

If I worked at a suicide hotline and failed another boy, there would probably be two of us dead. I wouldn't mess up my second attempt.

Out of nowhere, Tara asked me today about my reasons for attempting suicide. (That's maybe the first time I've called it that. I've been hiding behind euphemisms like doing myself harm or wanting to end my existence. I'm going to ask Doctor Chase if this development is as important as I suspect it might be.) I hemmed and hawed for a moment. Delilah and Nuncia sat quietly and looked out the window. Tara looked at me with fawn eyes.

I told them that I had been presented with an opportunity to genuinely help someone who was in very serious need of being helped, and that I failed at this.

Tara asked me if I had tried my best. Before I processed this, she went on to tell me that if I had, in fact, tried my best, there was nothing to be disappointed in myself about. From the mouths of babes.

From the Journal of
Delilah Duncan

I like the people I'm in here with this time. They know who I am, but just barely. There's a man who used to be a priest. He tried to kill himself by slitting his wrists. I'm going to go out on a limb and say that his childhood was pretty protective. Not a lot of sex, drugs or rock and roll in that boy's life. I think he said that he'd heard my music just to be polite. He's very quiet, more out of uncertainty than shyness. At least that's my read.

We have a young woman in here who has defied all the odds. Her story is fucking unbelievable. Born in a small village in Central America someplace, worked as a cook for a U.S. Embassy, cooked and kept house for an NBA player. This is all bat-shit crazy, right? She had a pretty upscale restaurant in Northern Virginia someplace, and it failed. Anyway, she's a suicide attempt, too.

And we have a couple of kids with addiction issues. God, the stories I could tell about watching this happen to people around me about a thousand times in my life. When it's easy as fuck to get pills or powders or booze, it's going to happen.

In a way, I'm lucky that my thing has always been alcohol. And thank goodness I have Dobro to look after me. He's great handling my money and all of that, but he's better at handling me. He seems to know just when I'm nearing the edge of a cliff and he shoots my fat ass back in this place.

The Panamanian girl is ballsy. Nobody walked her by the hand to where she got to. And she's often a little too outspoken at inappropriate times. She bitched at the little girl serving our lunch today. Granted, the food is not what anyone would call haute cuisine, but it's a mental hospital, for fuck's sake. And it certainly isn't the little girl's fault. All she's doing is shoveling it up.

So, I went to the Panamanian woman's room about an hour before lights out and sat on the edge of her bed and chatted with her. We talked about stuff that bothers us deep down and how that sometimes that stuff can come out when it's least expected. She was surprisingly receptive. I'm going to go out on a limb and guess that not a ton of people have talked to her this way. I mean, I get it that her life has not been one, smooth road from a shithole village in the jungle to owning a restaurant. I get it that she's had to deal with some crap along the way. And I'm sure she's had interpersonal issues like we all have. She's not unattractive, in an exotic kind of way. She has beautiful black hair and really expressive dark eyes, and a pretty nice little form to her...good tits like I used to have a hundred years ago. I'd be astounded if she hasn't had a boyfriend or two along the way.

Again, she was receptive. She even went so far as to walk down the hall to the priest's room and have a chat with him. He made a pretty fucking lame attempt at scolding her after the incident with the lunch girl. You can guess how that went down.

We sit around a big table for our meals, always in the same seating arrangement. Gabi, the girl who scoops out the food for everyone, brings me a tray of food every time she's working. I have a hell of a time carrying anything with these goddamn crutches, and a tray would be next to impossible.

I thought about it this morning, how I've had people wait on me and fetch shit for me for most of my life. When you hit it big in the music biz, they fawn all over you. The label, agents, fans, of course. They don't allow you to lift a finger. No wonder so many of us end up all twisted up in ourselves. How is that even close to healthy or normal?

My mother, may she rot in hell, took advantage of all of this. I was the one making all the dough, but she was the one who reveled in the lifestyle. I'd write a book about the awful shit she did, and did to me...her own daughter, but it would be too sad. It would open old wounds that need to remain healed.

I was actually approached a few years ago about writing a book. Well, the book guys assign someone to actually do the writing. They sit with a tape recorder and ask questions for about a week, and then they crap out some scandalous and poignant masterpiece they think will sell millions of copies because it has your name attached to it. Mine would be extra poignant in that I've supposedly got this MS type affliction, and because I've gotten so fat that I can hardly move. And I certainly can't sing any more. Not even in the tub when I'm alone.

I spoke with Dobro on the phone today. I don't know what I'd do without him. I'm glad he still enjoys the life, the business. He invites me to visit him in LA just about every time we talk. But that is all very much behind me at this point. Except for these little jaunts to this hospital for what he calls fine-tuning, I don't know if I'll ever really travel again. I'm comfortable in the mansion, as he calls it, and I have pretty decent people looking after me. I never feel like they're doing their jobs around the house for any reason other than a paycheck, but they're decent…like I said.

Dobro gets his cut, for sure, but I think he would still look out for me even if he didn't. And I have more money than I'll ever spend, believe me. Sell a few millions records and people line up to pay you. And to kiss your fat ass, of course.

Cass Elliot introduced me to him. Gosh, I haven't thought of her in years. What a talent. So outspoken and honest. And who would have ever thought that tiny and petite Delilah, with her smoking hot body and her skintight leathers would someday have as fat an ass as Cass. Sounds like a song lyric.

I was getting ready to divorce my first husband, the bass player. God, he was gifted in everything he did. And we had a really good thing going, too. He just had to walk away from time to time. No notice, no nothing. Just gone, sometimes for a month or more.

Dobro took over my finances and eventually took over my life. He supported me when I wanted to produce my own records and stood behind me when I went in different directions with my music. That was a gamble. I remember the uncertainty of all of that. But it worked out, and he was one of the reasons it did.

Two things tonight, and then I'm off to sleep. I notice that the priest, John, has started cleaning up everyone's tray after meals. It's a small gesture, but I'm going to guess it means something big to him. He does it quietly and without any fanfare. Everyone thanks him except for that boy Peter.

About Peter, he lost his shit today and had to be walked into another area. I'm guessing they shot him up with something to quiet him down. He's very unsettling to be around.

We had a field trip today. It should have been fun, but I just sat on one of the plastic chairs and watched the others. If I'd have even tried to limp my fat ass out there and roll a ball down the lane, it would have been an accident waiting to happen. Peter, of course, tried to fuck it all up by ordering a drink on his way to the bathroom. What could he possibly have been thinking? After he was busted, he sat and stewed for the entire rest of the time. They need to lobotomize that little prick.

It finally happened. Tara and that shithead Peter got busted doing the nasty. We all knew they had been doing it. You'd have to be blind not to notice that they were always late to meetings and meals. I mean, it's a rule that probably makes sense, but is there really any harm in it?

Tara was pretty shook up, and Peter, of course, was angry. They moved him to a different ward or something...a different part of the hospital. Once Tara settles down and relaxes, she'll be fine. She really has embraced the process of beating drugs, and that would be a shame to see that interrupted at all. I think I'll probably ask her to join Nuncia and me for our afternoon chats. I have a feeling, just from looking at Tara's parents, that her mother might be one of those women who keeps a nice house, drives the kids to the dentist and never expresses an opinion that might be different from her husband's. That's certainly not who I am, and it sure as shit isn't who Nuncia is. Maybe a bit of variety in the role model department will do Tara some good.

There is clearly a warm spot in hell for the man who got that kid hooked on heroin. I have seen it a hundred times where somebody suggests a new and different kind of high to a friend. That's horrible, but I can almost wrap my brain around it. But this guy was an adult man, and she was just a child. And the guy was in business with her dad…he was friends with her dad. How could anyone get that low? Men seem to be able to do just about anything for a good piece of ass. I certainly went through a lot of that when I was young. I grasp the concept, for sure. But this guy! He's Satan.

Nuncia asked the priest to sit with us in the afternoons. I guess no one new is joining our morning group sessions, so it was awkward having the three girls sit in the sunshine and shoot the shit, and to have the one man in the gang sitting all by himself. He reads quite a little bit, and the few times he adds something to the conversation, it can be pretty funny. He's the champion of self-deprecation. But it's genuine with him. I get the feeling that he truly believes he is worthless. And if I ever took myself out, it would not be by slitting my wrists. It might not be a bad way to go, but if you come up short in the attempt, the recovery looks like it's a bitch.

And, of course, now that the priest is sitting with us, we talk about sex. Oh well, he's a man like all other men. It's funny to me how we all just open up with our thoughts and emotions when we're sitting in the window versus how we react to Doctor Chase's questions in our group sessions. He's the authority figure, I guess, and that can be a bit daunting.

I talked a little bit about my marriages and about my introduction to sex through my mother pimping me out. That's an ugly way to put it, but it's accurate.

Nuncia and Tara had very little to say. Tara's young and Nuncia comes across like sex would be a low priority in her life. She hinted at the fact that something happened to her sister, that maybe she was raped or something back in the jungle. But she didn't open up about it very much. Maybe that will come later as she gets more comfortable with all of us.

Tara is a hot little ticket, though. For the life of me I don't know what she saw in that loser deadbeat kid. Maybe it was out of loneliness, or maybe she just wanted some little piece of her life in here to resemble the outside. Either way, she has a nice little body. That kid Peter never had it so good.

I know I wasn't the only one who wanted to ask the priest if he'd fucked around with any altar boys. I'm sorry, but it's in the news all the time. And why else would a priest try to off himself if not for something like that? I don't know what would be a more despicable crime, getting some teenage girl hooked on smack, or fiddling around with a little boy who trusts you. That's about as low as it gets.

I find it interesting that when we sit and chat looking out over the mountains, that we pretty much follow the same format as when we are in our group sessions with Doctor Chase. Someone, usually me, will bring up a subject, and then we go around our little circle and add our individual two cents to everything. Today we talked a lot about parents. Tara wins that contest hands down, and I am very certainly the loser. I went through a shit ton of therapy to somewhat come to grips with all the stuff I went through with my mother. When I look back on all of that, an eighteen year-old girl who had hit records overnight, traveling all over the world, literally, watching her mother fuck half the band and more than half of the tour guys, well it's pretty amazing that I didn't come out of it more screwed up than I was. Especially since my own introduction to sex, which should have been warm and exciting and kind of breathless, was really just all about manipulation. Add to all that the fact that my mother was *handling* my money, which was already a lot of money. I probably needed someone to take care of that. I was certainly in no position to make good decisions. Decisions that would have set me up for the future and all.

I thank my lucky stars for Dobro, and I told the gang this today. He saved me in more ways than one. All the time my mother was telling me that he was just trying to get his hands on our money…*our money*… he was actually making moves to get her hands off it. Want to have a shit year? Interrupt your tour and your whole career and then drag your mother through court. But in the end, it worked out. Dobro took over the finances, made a ton of investments…I own a lot of stuff that generates a lot of revenue, even outside the royalties from all those songs and records. But really more importantly, Dobro saw that I was in trouble emotionally. He saw that I was already drinking way too much, and that my lifestyle was not one that was going to be much good for me in the long run. And how crazy is it that I met him at a cocktail party? Cass was there and introduced us. One of those boring-as-shit parties the label puts on so that they can bring potential investors up close and personal with the talent. That's me. Delilah Duncan. The talent.

I've been pretty open about why I'm here. I'm fat. This supposed disease I have. I go on binges of feeling sorry for myself and drink way too much. And Tara has been open about why she's in here. Poor kid. I just don't see her smile a hell of a lot. It's like she has a blackness to her on the inside, and she just tries to keep it there.

Nuncia and Father Dud, this is what we all are calling him now, are far more guarded. I'm not going to say that suicide never once crossed my mind. It probably has with most people, at least once. But that is such a deep and powerful hole you have to be in to go down that road. Talk about permanent, right? And the deeper the hole, the more personal the reasons for getting there, I suppose.

So, out of the blue, Tara asks Father Dud why he slit his wrists. Even Nuncia's ears perked up a little. He said that he had been in a position to help someone who needed his help, and that he was unable to. Tara asked him if he had done his best to try to help, and he said that he didn't know, that he was still thinking about that. I read somewhere that most people who survive a suicide attempt end up not killing themselves. I don't know if this is because they get therapy, or whatever. But I don't know if this will be the case with Dud. Whatever drove him into that hole still seems to be pushing. That's a mangled metaphor, but I know what I mean.

Peter

When Delilah, Nuncia, Tara and Dud shuffled into the large meeting area, they were surprised to find Peter sitting beside Doctor Chase. He wore the same clothing, had the same disheveled hair, the same slippers. But he was changed. The twitchiness and edginess that he seemed always to carry in his pockets were gone. He did not make eye contact with anyone. This would have necessitated him looking up from his slippers, and he did not do this.

"Welcome back," said the priest.

"Yeah, welcome back, Peter," echoed Delilah.

Nuncia sat in her usual place and folded her hands in her lap. Tara placed her hand on Peter's shoulder before moving to her chair. Inaudibly, she mouthed the words *I'm sorry* to him.

"Well, as everyone has noticed, we have Peter back with us. And I'm very happy about that. Peter, do you have anything you would like to say to the group this morning?"

The young man looked up for the first time. There had always been a look of disdain on his face, as if the flavor of the air he was breathing was not pleasing to him. That look was absent. He portrayed no emotion now; his visage was a blank canvas, new-fallen snow in an untrampled field. His eyes were glassed and appeared unable to focus clearly on anything. Although Delilah, over the course of her many visits to this place, had seen patients drugged into a more submissive state of being, it was Tara who looked immediately sick to her stomach. She knew what it was like to be a stranger in one's own body, to be feeling and sensing things, but in a completely different way, to be unable to connect the dots between sensation and movement, to be floating in an ether neither good nor bad, but certainly different. And she took ownership of the fact that Peter was now in this place.

"I want to say I'm sorry for disrupting the group," said Peter with a voice the others did not recognize.

He had been brash but was now beaten. There exists a fine line between bravado and insecurity, and Peter now was very clearly nowhere near it.

Edward Chase watched attentively for the other patients' reactions. Empathy from Tara and John Dudley was good; a deeper dive into her own self by Nuncia was not. Delilah seemed not to care either way.

The session was unremarkable, as Doctor Chase asked each of the patients to offer up an example of a process they would change when they left the hospital.

"A series of processes, or steps, are taken by each of us every day. Some of those, in each our lives, can lead to bad decisions, bad habits. It can be very helpful to identify some of them."

"Thinking of my dead sister, that's what got me in here," said Nuncia. "Should I not think about her?"

"No. That's not what I'm saying," said Edward. "I'm sure you have many wonderful memories of your sister, as well as some not-so-good images. What might help in this case would be to think about your role in the dynamic. It bothers you that by not being able to help your sister financially, that she found herself in harm's way. So, you might want to think about whether or not you had any options at that time. Whether or not you did your best. And I'm guessing you probably did your best, but circumstances prevented that from being good enough."

"Circumstances made the fucking animals that raped her because my father couldn't keep paying them protection money, that's what circumstances made."

Nuncia stood and walked towards the doorway leading to the patients' rooms. She turned back to the group. For the first time since being in the hospital, she was crying.

"And they made her drink bleach. The little bit of money that my father had, because I couldn't send him anymore, he used it to buy alcohol and get drunk. So, they punished him by making his daughter drink bleach. After they abused her body."

"Nuncia, please come back and join us," said Doctor Chase.

"So, maybe I'll just stop thinking about my beautiful little sister burning her throat to death. Maybe that will work."

She left the sitting area and walked quickly to her room. The other patients sat in silence as they processed. Nuncia, for the first time, was as vulnerable as all of them. The street-wise smartass that had been the subject of brashness and amusement to them was now changed. She was wounded, as they all were, and she fought with the same demons they all did.

"No wonder she tried to off herself," said Delilah.

"Let's take a ten minute break," said Doctor Chase. "I want to check on Nuncia."

That afternoon, after lunch was eaten and John Dudley had cleared away trays and plastic silverware from everyone's place at the table, the group sitting in the window convened as usual. Peter remained alone on the far side of the large and brightly lit room.

Nuncia sat with one leg tucked under her. She had returned with Doctor Chase to the group session she had earlier walked out of but seemed rather noticeably changed since sharing the horrible events of her sister's death. She now possessed, in the eyes of her fellow patients, a fragility that had not been present before. It had been a stretch for each of them to believe that Nuncia had attempted suicide, but it was not now.

"If all of you will excuse me this afternoon, I'm going to go sit next to Peter and see if he wants to talk," said John Dudley. "I feel bad, him sitting all alone over there."

"He's probably going to tell you to fuck off, Dud," said Delilah. "But go ahead. It's a nice thing to do."

The priest walked slowly to the group of chairs where Peter was sitting. This was an unusual step for him; typically, when discussions were had, it was a person or persons coming to him. He almost never initiated the dialogue.

"Mind if I sit with you for a little bit?" he asked the boy.

Peter shrugged.

John sat loudly in a chair opposite the boy. He took a deep and audible breath in through his nose. He folded his hands as if in prayer as he exhaled. He took note of the vacant stare. It was as if Peter was incapable of focusing on anything, but only by a fraction. He seemed now to be mentally and physically spent. Exhausted so completely that thought was impossible, that thinking now demanding too much effort.

"If you would rather be left alone, Peter, I'll certainly honor that," he said. "But I thought you might want to shoot the breeze a little. We haven't seen you in a few days, and I thought you might want me to catch you up on how everyone is doing."

"Whatever you want," said Peter.

"What a horrible thing to learn from Nuncia this morning, right?" asked John.

Peter nodded.

"So, what have you been doing the last few days?" asked John.

"The same. Just mostly by myself. I talked with a couple other doctor types, but not much other than that. They have me on medication now."

"How's that working?" asked the priest. "How you feeling?"

"I don't. I don't feel much of anything."

"That's probably temporary," said Dudley. "That's probably just to calm you down a little, do you think?"

"I don't know," said the boy. "I don't care."

"Well, we're glad to have you back with us. I'm glad. It's nice to have another man in the group. I've been terribly outnumbered."

Peter nodded but said nothing. The priest's words were reaching him but had little meaning. As if he was hearing all of this in a foreign language.

"My wrists are itching like crazy," said Dudley. "I guess that's a sign that I'm healing. At least the wrists are healing. I can't tell if the rest of me is."

This offering up of an intimate detail was textbook counseling. As a young man, Dudley was certain that he wanted to be a priest, but the fear of dealing with parishioners' personal lives never left him. He had completed a great deal of course-work in psychology, and that had helped. But he very clearly was not a natural. Had he been a musician, he would never have been able to play without the sheet music perched on the piano ledge in front of him.

"Why did you?" asked Peter without looking up.

"Why did I slice my wrists open?"

The boy nodded. He glanced at the priest for an instant before looking down again.

Dudley again took a deep breath in through his nose. In the two seconds before exhaling, he considered walking away. He did not know why he had felt it important to sit with the boy, nor did he have a clue as to what to do next. The thought crossed his mind that this action was some sort of contrition on his part, some noble effort to assuage the guilt he felt for his actions, or lack of action, in the past. He nodded to himself as he exhaled.

"There was a little boy," he said. "He was a perfect little kid, about ten years old. He was an altar boy at my church, the church I worked at. He was a little goofy, but very polite. Very well behaved."

John Dudley inched his chair a bit closer to Peter's. If he was going to go down this path, he wanted to be able to use the softest voice he possessed. Peter continued to look down, but the priest could see that his eyes were opened wide.

"This little boy came to me and told me that something horrible was happening to him. He did this in confession on a Saturday morning."

"What happened to him?" asked Peter without looking up.

"Not to candy-coat it, but he was being sexually abused by one the older priests. It had been going on for several weeks, and the little boy was afraid or embarrassed to go to his parents or any of his teachers. There's a certain anonymity in confessing one's sins to a priest. If you've never seen it, the whole process takes place in a darkened closet and there's a shaded screen separating us. So, I think as a last resort, the little boy told me."

"What did you do?" asked the boy.

"I prayed. I prayed for guidance as to what to do. The priest was an older man. Although I knew deep down that the boy was probably telling me the truth…allegations of this sort were really coming out of the woodwork about then…I was unsure of what action to take. So, I prayed. And I allowed an older man, a man for whom I had held great respect but now questioned, bully me into silence."

John Dudley was sweating. His shirt was wet under his armpits and down the entirety of the center of his back. The sound of his voice was coming from vocal cords made of fine-grain sandpaper. He could feel his heart beats in his reddened ears.

"But my prayers were not answered," he whispered. "The little boy, the beautiful little laughing boy, committed suicide. He trusted me and I failed him. I failed everyone."

"I feel bad for you, man," said Peter. "I really do."

After a moment of collection, the priest placed his hand on Peter's shoulder. But only for an instant.

"We all feel bad in here," he said. "For ourselves, but also, hopefully, for each other. Does that make sense?"

Peter did not look up, but his back straightened slightly. His posture told the priest that what he had just heard about feeling bad for each other had registered. Dudley had been wrong before. By his own thinking, he was wrong more often than right. But this seemed like it was real. The boy had reacted, and this told the priest that something good had just transpired.

"Not a lot makes sense to me right now," said Peter. "But I think I know what you mean, and I do feel bad for you."

"Thank you. And I feel bad for you, too. I don't know your story, Peter, but I'd be glad to listen if you ever want to talk things out. It can make us feel better. I feel better, even just sharing that stuff about the little boy. It's hard talking about that stuff, but it's almost always good to do it."

"How did he do it?" asked Peter.

"He hanged himself from a beam in his family's garage."

"What was his name?"

"Adam. His name was Adam."

"How's the Cat Woman?"

Edward and Millie were driving to a resort in the mountains for a weekend get-a-way. Millie was fully into her third week of classes, and Edward had surprised her

97

with this mini-vacation. She sat in the passenger seat, her bare feet resting on the dash, snow boots and socks on the car floor beneath her. Edward spoke without looking away from the road.

"She's good. You know, Edward, at first, I was reluctant to keep seeing her, but we've kind of hit a groove, she and I. She's goofy. I get all of that. Especially to someone in your lofty position of knowing everything about the human body and psyche. But she's very soothing."

"One, I'm far from knowing everything about anything. Two, what's the secret to her success?"

"I think it's personal. I don't mean that it's personal in a *none of your business* way. It's personal in that she's soothing to me for reasons that might not apply to someone else. For me, it's that I continued seeing her because the expectations were so low. I wasn't…I don't want to use the word *intimidated* by her…it was more that I didn't expect anything big to happen, so any little development was a welcome surprise. Does that make sense?"

Edward placed his right hand on his wife's shoulder for a moment before returning it to the steering wheel.

"I makes a lot of sense, Mil. If your expectations were low and you felt like you had some success in figuring some things out, then that success would kind of propel you forward. It makes sense that these little successes would put you in a comfort zone with her. I'm glad."

"What kind of food does this place have. I want a really nice dinner and some good wine," said Millie.

"There's a top shelf steak and seafood place connected with the resort. Very good reviews."

They checked in at four in the afternoon. Millie poured a hot bath and sprinkled in red bath beads. Edward changed into workout clothes and headed to the gym.

"I'll be back in a few," he said.

Millie, standing naked in the doorway to the bathroom, cocked her hip, as if posing somewhat provocatively for him. Her dark hair fell over her eyes. Her pubic hair was untrimmed.

"Don't be long please," she said.

"If I ever get to the point where I prefer the gym to your body, Mil, call an ambulance. And a shrink."

The weekend was as relaxing a time as the two had shared in many, many months. The food was delicious, and the resort offered spectacular views from its many hiking and walking trails. The elevation was just high enough for the light dusting of snow to remain in the valley and on the mountain sides. After some debate, the Chases had decided to bring their warm weather clothing from Rochester when they moved south, and it proved useful throughout the weekend as they explored a new trail with each outing.

"How are things at work?" Millie asked as they moved methodically up a rise filled with pine trees.

Her breath was visible in the cold air.

"They're alright. This one group...the ones I've talked a little about...they're making some progress, but only baby steps. They were completely self-oriented at first, and that's normal. But I've seen them opening up to each other a little, and that's good. It's just so bloody slow sometimes. You want to see that development, but it's hard to remain patient."

"Does it ever not happen? Do they ever *never* get out of being self-oriented, as you say?"

"Unfortunately, yes. And I have one of those in this group. A young man who seems incapable of seeing anything around him with anything except angry eyes."

"That's very poetic, Edward."

They continued their climb through the pine trees and rested on a ledge over-looking the valley below. This part of the Appalachian chain had not yet been discovered by wealthy home-builders looking for pristine areas in which to rough it. Mountain life with cappuccino and jacuzzi. The sun was resting at the top of a mountain across the valley from their perch.

Blue smoke snaked up from the chimneys attached to the small houses below. They had been built along the river at the bottom of the valley, and had no doubt stood for years. Edward and Millie had passed them just before heading up the steep and winding road to the resort. Children playing outside in clothing most certainly incapable of keeping them warm, tossed snowballs at Edward's car as he drove past.

"It has its own kind of scenic beauty, doesn't it?" asked Edward.

"No denying that," Millie answered. "I wonder what they do for a living, the people living in those cabins down there."

"They probably work at the resort. I don't think there's a lot of mining going on anymore. I don't know."

"Let's go back," she said. "I don't want to be hiking up here after it gets too dark to see,"

After they had returned to their room, and after they had removed their clothing and made very comfortable, very relaxed love, Millie slipped out from under the covers and proclaimed first use of the shower.

"Can I join you?" her husband asked.

"Nope. I want some self-oriented time to get clean."

He laced his fingertips behind his head as he lay back on his pillow and smiled.

When Millie had stepped out of the steamed bathroom, white fluffy bathrobe and towel wrapped around her hair, she announced that the shower was now his. He adored his wife, just then and there, more than he thought he ever had. Her feet were delicate, her legs were those of a dancer, her eyes shone brightly enough to melt a glacier.

And when he had finished his shower and stood drying himself with another of the huge towels, he peeked into the travel bag his wife had left on the counter beside the sink. Despite a long-professed aversion to using pills as a method of birth control, Millie had taken them religiously since the loss of their child. Edward knew better than to look. He knew that this was an invasion of his wife's privacy and that it was wrong. And the euphoria he secretly anticipated at the prospect of not finding the small plastic circle containing one pill for each day of the month was replaced by a minor dejection at seeing it. But he deserved it; he had earned it by not being respectful of his wife's space, and he knew that.

It was a warming day in late-December when Dr. Chase first mentioned the prospect of some or all of the patients in his group going home.

"I asked for each of you to put some thought into what actions you decide to take that might be different after leaving here than when you entered. There's a reason for that. I think all of us understand that. Probably not a great idea to go on doing the exact same stuff in the exact same order, right?"

The thought of walking out of the Botetourt State Hospital impacted each of the patients differently, to be sure. To Delilah, it was nothing new. This was her third session of getting "fine-tuned" in the words of her manager Dobro. She would go home to her beautiful house, eat meals prepared by her hired cook, and bathe in her large and clam-shaped bathtub. She would make some effort to watch the drinking, but she knew that it would be a transitory effort at best.

Tara also had a home to return to. Her parents had not missed a visitation opportunity, and she knew that they would remain supportive throughout her continued struggle with addiction. She had been on a mild dose of a drug intended to fight the craving to get high, and she knew that her mother would keep a close eye on her to make certain she continued on with it. Her father would smile and would provide a truly unlimited supply of positive reinforcement. The last time she had gone through this, it was almost tempting to shoot up just to interrupt the endless stream of his voice promising a rosy future.

"I'm going to go into a half-way house for another month. They test your blood alcohol every day, and if you blow positive, they kick your ass out. After that, I'll probably try to go home and see what's what. Maybe find somebody who will let me crash with them until I figure stuff out"

This was Peter sharing his plans with Father Dud as they sat in the day room after lunch.

"That sounds like a good plan," said John.

He waited for Peter to offer up more details.

"I really just want to feel normal again," he said after a moment. He had not shaved in days, and the very light, very thin hair on his face made him look younger than he really was. Boy trying to grow a beard.

"I suspect they'll wean you off of whatever it is they are giving you," said Dud. "I would certainly think that's the protocol."

Again, the priest waited, but without appearing to be eager for more discussion. He nodded as if digesting deep thought.

"You want to hear something crazy?" asked Peter.

"We're in a mental hospital," said Dud. "How can anything any of us say not sound at least a little crazy?"

And the priest who had very cautiously and quietly attempted to befriend this young man over the past several afternoons saw, for the first time, a smile. John Dudley's victories in life were small and seldom. But this connection, the glint of hope that he might be on to something in his effort to engage the boy, this most certainly made the list.

"I was thinking of joining the Marines," said Peter.

"Wow," said Dud. "That's not what I was expecting to hear. That's certainly a life-changing decision, Peter. Why the Marines?"

"A guy in the other wing of the hospital, when I was over there after getting busted with Tara, he used to be in the Marines. He told me they give you structure. You know, discipline kind of structure. Maybe I need some of that."

Again, the priest nodded. He peeked at the girls' triangle of chairs across the room. He wondered, only for an instant, what they were talking about.

"That's a big step, isn't it? Have you spoken to Dr. Chase about it?"

"Yeah. He didn't chime in one way or the other. He just told me to take my time and give it a lot of thought before committing. You know, I've never been anywhere. I went to a fucking beach in Indiana once with my family before all of us started to hate each other. It might be nice to see some of the world."

"That's pretty sound advice he gave you, at least in my opinion."

"And he wants me to continue working towards the root cause of why I drink the way I do. He harps on that shit every time I talk to him."

Dud could feel it. He could see the first subtle tracings of light coming up in the eastern sky. That the boy had raised the issue on his own, this was truly something. The priest waited quietly. His heart pounded.

"I know the root cause, by the way," said Peter. "I'll tell you, if you want me to."

"If you feel like it, Peter. You know what you and I talk about stays between us."

After an agonizing silence, Peter put his hand to his face. He was failing in a strained effort to keep himself from crying.

"The little boy you told me about, Adam? What happened to him, happened to me. I'm guessing he was molested by some priest, and that, because you didn't help him…were not able to help him, that's why you're in here.

Molested. Thant's a nice way of putting it, isn't it? That's what happened to me. When I was thirteen. Two older boys. On my way walking home from school. In their car."

Dud lowered his head and held it in his meaty hands. He began to sweat, and he felt moisture in the center of his back. He called up a picture of the boy Adam sitting in the darkened confessional closet, a screen between his face and that of his redeemer, his savior, his protector, the All-and-Powerful Father Dud. He recognized, truly for the first time, the courage the boy Adam, and now the boy Peter, had possessed to be able to speak these horrific words. He saw the courage as a brilliantly white light, and he knew that he would never be one to project light like this.

He also knew not to ask a question. Peter was fighting hard to hold in the tears and emotion that seemed now to want to flood out; a deluge held back for many years by a dam constructed from pain, anger and a sense of abandonment. The priest placed one hand on the boy's shoulder. He did not look back at the women sitting opposite him. The fear that he might make eye contact at this instant of intensity with any of them kept his vision straight down. He lacked the courage to connect, even for an instant and from across the room, with any of them.

"That's a horrible thing that was done to you, Peter. I marvel at your courage and your strength," he finally said.

Peter sneered and shook his head, adopting an aloof countenance in an effort not to cry.

"That's not it," he said. "The thing is that I went back several times. I got in their car a bunch more times when I didn't have to."

The priest took several seconds to gather himself.

"This is not a sin," he said in a whisper. "This is nothing you've done wrong, Peter. This is only people being people. There's no roadmap to what is right and what is wrong. No sign along the path telling us that we did something we should have not done. You did what you felt. No harm to anyone came from that. Don't pass judgement on yourself. What you elected to do was perhaps the thing you should have done. Use no one else's eyes to see that. Only your eyes."

Peter and the priest talked in trivialities over the course of the next few days. The big ticket items they had shared with each other had created a connection that allowed for casual chatter, back and forth. Peter wanted to know about Dud's time at seminary; Dud was genuinely interested in Peter's idea of joining the Marines.

"If we are to believe what we hear, the basic training is quite a challenge," said Dud.

"I could do it. I played football in high school, and I've been in about twenty fights already in my life. I'm tough enough."

"I don't have any doubt of that," said the priest. "I don't think you'd have any problem with the psychological element, either. Who knows? You might really find your calling in the service. I've had parishioners, quite a few, actually, whose kids made careers out of the military."

"Maybe," said Peter. "But I have to get out of here and get through the half-way house first. I might talk to a recruiter when I get to the half-way house."

"I'd like it if you kept in touch with me, Peter."

"Where are you going to go?" asked the boy.

"I'm working on that. The diocese I used to be under has offered to let me stay at one of its parishes for a brief time, until I can figure out where else to go. When I did this to myself, I had been living in a small apartment in the little town where my church was located. I was working at a grocery store. I might think about going back there. I'm not sure. You don't make a lot of money as a priest, believe me. But I don't need much to get by"

"Can I ask you something personal?"

"Of course, you can. We've certainly shared enough to allow for that, haven't we?"

Peter nodded and looked at the mountains.

"Are you feeling…I don't know…are you feeling confident that you're not going to try to do yourself in again?"

"Don't take this the wrong way, but I hope you and I never see each other in here again. Does that make sense?"

"Yeah. God, I'll be glad to get out of here, won't you?"

Both men looked towards the women as they noticed Tara walking to them. She was delicate and walked with the pants of her hospital scrubs dragging the ground. Her slippers were not visible.

"I just wanted to let you both know that I'm leaving here tomorrow. My parents want me home for Christmas, and Doctor Chase thinks it'll be okay for me as long as I continue seeing someone after I'm out. I just wanted to say bye."

"Good luck to you, Tara. I will certainly hold you in my prayers," said the priest.

"Thank you. I need all the prayers I can get," she said.

"I'm sorry if I got you in trouble, Tara," said Peter. "But that was a lot of fun."

John Dudley had seen that Tara carried a darkness with her, at times blacker than others. But the smile she could not contain just now brightened her features and warmed the two men.

"Sorry you have to hear this, Father, but I had a lot of fun, too, Peter."

Peter was the next to go. The day after New Year's Day he was driven in a hospital van to a half-way house on the outskirts of Roanoke. The plan was for him to live there with five other men and an administrator, himself a recovering alcoholic. He wore the same clothes he had worn on the morning he was transported from a detention ward of the hospital to Botetourt. He was given a toothbrush, a travel-size tube of mint toothpaste and a razor by the orderly who walked him out the door. Mouthwash was conspicuously not included in the travel package.

Over the course of the next thirty days, he would be counseled by a social worker and plans for his next steps in life would be developed. His breath would be tested for alcohol once per day. If he failed even one of these tests, he would be asked to immediately leave the home.

"They call that a *dirty house*," he explained to the priest.

"What would happen to you in that event? In the event they asked you to leave?"

"You see these people in homeless shelters? These people sleeping in bus stations and stuff like that? That'd be me."

This scenario bothered John Dudley to the point of near nausea. In his own life, before entering seminary, he had possessed so very little independence and worldliness that the notion of being out on his own was terrifying. Let alone not having a bed to sleep in or food to eat. The notion of this young person walking the streets looking for help of any kind was almost more than the priest could bear.

"Please don't let that happen, Peter. Could you go home to your parents in that event?"

The boy shook his head.

"That bridge burned a long time ago," he said.

"Let me give you the address of the parish I was under," he said. "I'm not sure where I'll be, but you might be able to reach me through them in the event you needed something. I'm not sure I'd even be in a position to be of any help to you, Peter. But I'd feel better knowing that you at least had that address."

"Have a little faith, John," said the boy.

It was the first time he had used the priest's given name, and it struck him as a sign of confidence.

With the kids gone, the troika of Delilah, Nuncia and Dud resumed their chatting sessions in the window looking out towards the mountains. To a person, each of them had felt a tinge of responsibility for Tara and Peter; mothering and fathering children none of them had. Now that they were gone, a sense of calm hung in the air as the three talked. Even Father Dud removed himself from his self-constructed shell more and more often.

"You know, if Peter drinks even one time over the next thirty days, he'll be kicked out of that half-way house. What's worse is that he has no place to go in that event. His parents apparently want nothing to do with him."

"So much for a safety net," said Delilah. She was sitting in the chair she had claimed upon arrival at the hospital; assigned seating without the name cards. The movement of her right hand, forward and back as if scratching an itch on her thigh, was almost undiscernible to the others. They had grown used to it.

"He was talking about going into the Marines after he gets through his thirty days. Some guy in another part of the hospital here planted that seed."

"Yeah, like the Marine soldiers won't ever corrupt him into drinking," said Nuncia. "I've seen them come in restaurants I worked at, and they can be very loud and get very drunk."

"It's not about the drinking with Peter," said Dud. "The drinking was only a symptom. I really believe that he addressed the real issue a couple of times in the past week or so. At least a little bit. All we can do is pray and hope for the best for him, right?"

"You can pray, Father. That's your specialty," said Nuncia. "I don't have anybody to pray to anymore."

The priest nodded and rubbed his chin. His was not a position to speak to Nuncia's lack of faith, and he knew this. His own faith had been tested; he had retained his belief in God, but it had been altered. His God was not omniscient nor judicial; his God left a lot of the dirty work to the people grinding away at life below Him. His God was still a shining light, but the light was less bright.

"What's his deal?" asked Delilah.

"I'm not sure," answered the priest. This was a lie he felt comfortable in telling, and that Delilah accepted knowingly.

The three sat in the sunlight, the only sound being that of Delilah's hand and arm moving continuously front to back on her leg.

"Does your disease bother you?" Nuncia asked.

"What disease?" Delilah answered.

"This disease that makes your hand move all the time. Your MS disease, or whatever it's called. Does it bother you? Does it hurt you?"

"I don't have any disease," said Delilah. "This is all a big scam. I can tell you two this because the chances that you'll tell anyone are nil. And because I absolutely wouldn't give two fucks about it even if you did tell someone."

Dud was looking at Delilah's lap. Nuncia's mouth was opened slightly.

"I don't understand," said Nuncia. "How is this a scam? What do you mean?"

"OK. I'll tell you," said Delilah as she shifted her very large rump in her chair.

"It was years ago, a hundred years ago. I was getting fat and my voice was losing its zing, and Dobro and I just thought it might be time to walk away from the business. I really didn't like it anymore…too many kids with zero fucking talent coming along and mass-producing shitty albums that sold like crazy. It was depressing, and I wanted out. So, I started telling anyone who asked me about it, about leaving the industry, that I was being forced to because of some un-named disease. Maybe I was seeking sympathy; maybe I was just fucking with the establishment kind of thing. But I started moving my hand like this whenever I was around anyone. Hand to God, after a while, it took more effort to stop it than to continue. So, yeah, I don't have a real disease. This is just something stupid I cooked up to promote the brand of Delilah Duncan. Stupid, huh?"

Nuncia and John Dudley smiled throughout Delilah's revelation. They both looked down at the large woman's lap as if the words they were hearing were originating there.

"That's crazy," said Nuncia. "That's some crazy shit, Delilah."

Another long silence consumed each of them. This had become routine. Subject changes did not ever flow from statement to statement; they were not inspired by something someone said. New topics came from contemplation percolated during the down time.

"I think that boy Peter had a real thing for Tara," said Father Dud. "I think he was truly sorry to see her leave, and that he had genuine concern for her future."

"I've seen that happen just about every time I'm in here," said Delilah. "Especially with kids, although not always with kids. They just have to get some, I guess."

"Their bodies screaming out to each other," said Nuncia. "They have to answer that craving."

Dud shuffled in his seat.

"I wouldn't know," he said. "I guess I just wouldn't know."

"So, you never had sex, Dud? Asked Delilah. "Even before you took your vows and all of that?"

The large priest shook his head.

"You ever diddle around with one of those altar boys?" asked Nuncia. "*There*, she said rather loudly, "I finally get the courage to ask you that."

"No," he said. "This is a very private matter, but I've never had any form of sex with another person."

"You should," said Delilah. "It's not healthy, it's not the way we're wired to never get laid. I bet it would make you feel like a new man. Really."

Father Dud chuckled and shook his head.

"Maybe I'll try it sometime," he said in an effort to dismiss the subject.

"You should do him," Delilah said to Nuncia. "Kind of a social experiment. You're young and have that smokin' body. Don't think you can hide it under those scrubs. I see those tits. You should do him, just once so he can see what all the fuss is about. It would be your gift to humanity."

Delilah Duncan was smiling throughout this suggestion. Dud felt his ears turning red. Nuncia adopted the look of disinterest they all had come to recognize as a self-protective force field.

"Alright," she said. "You want to give it a try, Father Dud? You want to see what the whole world knows? You game?"

"I wouldn't have the first idea as to how to do anything," said the priest. His discomfort was real but was now tinged with a subtle but recognizable hint of arousal. His mind flashed for an instant to the girls who had tied him to a tree as a boy. His guilt at even thinking these thoughts began to bubble up, but he fought through and actually enjoyed the moment.

"It's pretty straightforward," said Delilah.

"You put your thing in my thing," shrugged Nuncia.

That evening after dinner the troika convened outside Nuncia's room. John Dudley had showered twice and had flossed and brushed his teeth. He wore a fresh-out-of-the-laundry set of hospital scrubs. His nervousness was palpable; he was certain that his voice would crack in the event he attempted to speak. Delilah had asked about birth control, but Nuncia declared that she was very close to starting her period.

"Dud will be washed away," she said.

Nuncia was wearing the same hospital scrubs she always wore, but she appeared to wear them differently. The priest did not stare. He looked quickly at her bottom as she preceded him from the hallway into her room. He could count on one hand the number of occasions in the entirety of his life that he had allowed himself this indulgence…looking at a woman's body, even clothed.

"I'll stand out here and watch for anyone who might come by," said Delilah as she leaned against the wall, arms enclosed by her crutches.

"Do you want a chair?" asked Dud. "That can get uncomfortable for you standing like that, can't it?"

"Like it's going to take a long time," Nuncia said with a sneer. "You're going to squirt in twenty seconds," she said to the priest.

No noises, no muffled voices or bumping of headboards against the wall came from the room as Delilah Duncan stood sentry in the hallway. Approximately four minutes after the door had been shut, it opened as Father Dud emerged. He appeared unchanged. Delilah would not have guessed that his clothes had just been removed and then placed back on his rather large body. For a moment, she wondered if they had actually gone through with it. Maybe one or both of them had reconsidered and decided to abort the experiment.

This thought was eradicated as soon as she caned herself into Nuncia's room. Nuncia was standing beside her bed wearing only the bottom half of her hospital uniform. Her breasts were on display for the flash of a moment it took her to put her top on. There was no embarrassment and no rush.

Delilah sat on the side of the now unmade bed.

"Well, how was that?" she asked without looking at Nuncia.

"You know," said Nuncia, "for a priest, he has a pretty big one."

Delilah Duncan was in the home stretch of her latest stay at Botetourt. It had been more of an adventure, this trip, than any she had experienced before. She hoped that it might be her last, but she was relatively certain that it would not be. She felt good but she also looked forward to getting home and having a glass of red wine.

The head nurse at Botetourt had set her up in a tiny waiting room equipped with a desk and two chairs. She sat with her right hand and forearm resting on the desk, the circular and almost involuntary movement nearly subsided.

She dialed her manager's number from heart.

"Dobro Temple's office," said the young Californian woman who sat in the entry-way outside her boss's door.

"Hey, it's Delilah. Dobro around?"

"Yes, ma'am. Let me see if he can talk now. Hold for one sec."

Delilah knew that she got the treatment when she called. She knew that the more common answer to the question she had just asked, as to whether or not Dobro was around, would have been that he's in conference or that he's with a client. But she was Delilah Duncan, and the woman in California, probably young and sunny, knew to get her boss on the phone as quickly as possible. Even all these years after formally retiring, Delilah's royalties far out-paced any of Dobro's other clients. Dobro's cut of her earnings remained the largest single source of income he took in. This had been explained to the receptionist on the occasion of an earlier call.

"Delilah?" he said. "You alright?"

"Yeah, I'm fine. Getting ready to get out of here and head back to the mansion."

"How you feeling?"

"Like I want a hot bath and a glass of wine. I feel like I always feel."

"You need me to come out there? Just say the word and I'm on my way to the airport."

Delilah opened the drawer of the desk at which she was sitting. No pens, no pencils, no paperclips. Certainly, no scissors.

"No, but thanks for the offer, Dobro. I want to run something by you. Not as my manager, but as my friend. I have an idea."

"I have always acted more as your friend than as your manager, Delilah. I hope you know that."

"I do," she said.

She could picture him at his desk all those miles away in California. His gray hair would be tousled, he would be leaning back in the old and ragged swivel chair he refused to replace, his feet might rest on his desk. Despite dressing for comfort, almost always seen in jeans and a tee shirt, Dobro Temple wore dress shoes every day of his life.

He had rescued Delilah all those years ago, and she had repaid him with loyalty unknown in the client-agent dynamic. He had hired the right attorney to take back her sizable fortune from the mother who had attempted to abscond with it, and he had seen to it that she had remained out of the downward spiral that seemed to suck so many of the rich and famous down the drain. Shrinks, doctors, spiritual mentors, rehab resorts, ashrams. Delilah Duncan was helped by all of them along her path up the mountain to fame and fortune, and then again as she voluntarily retreated down to earth. And Dobro Temple was the man behind the support systems she had always found at her fingertips. He loved the income he derived from her; he loved the woman more.

"So, what's on your mind?" he asked. "Wait," he injected, "before we get into that, can I please interest you in a quick trip out here? Get you out of the cold weather for a few days?"

"No, but thanks," she said. "I want to get home. It's been a kooky month."

"Okay, okay. But you know the offer stands. You can stay at my place anytime you want for as long as you want."

"That's a good lead-in to my idea, Dobro. There are a couple of younger people at the hospital here with me. One is a guy who used to be a priest. The other is a woman whose story you would not believe. Came to America all alone as a child and lived the most unpredictable life you could imagine. I'll tell you all about it when we get a chance to talk after I'm home. Her story would make a great movie."

"What's the idea?" asked Dobro.

He had placed a pad of yellow legal paper on his lap and picked up the expensive Monte Blanc pen that had been given to him years ago by David Bowie. Although he never represented the rock star, he had done some sort of favor for him. Dobro loved the pen and actually used it. On this occasion, he suspected a laundry list of action items to be coming his way from across the telephone wires. Delilah rarely asked him for help, but when she did the requests could be detailed to a granular level.

"I'm thinking of having them both out to the mansion for a little bit. Quite honestly, Dobro, they have very few options for when they walk out of this place. You'd think that there would be some sort of fucking safety net for them, but there isn't. I think they're just going to send them back to where they came from with a pat on the ass and a wish for good luck. Anyway, you're always telling me that I have too much house for just one person, so I'm thinking of offering them a place to crash. At least for a while. Until they get some real options."

Dobro was drawing on his legal pad. A stick woman, a stick man, a stick woman blessed with a large tummy and a pair of crutches, a house, a dog and a hangman's noose.

"So, what are your thoughts?" asked Delilah.

"My first thought is that I love you for your kindness. My second thought is that you've lost your goddamn mind in that hospital this time. Two of them is bad enough. But two people coming out of a mental hospital? Think about the responsibility of that, Delilah. Is that a path you need to go down? Why don't you just have me have someone contact them on your behalf. Get them set up someplace safe and warm. Maybe pay a few bills for them. That's a couple of phone calls. I could get into that this afternoon if you want."

At the bottom of the page Dobro had begun making a list. Cities, apartments, lease, power, water, etc. He scribbled the word *salary* but quickly scratched it out.

"I thought of that, Dobro. But these people have helped me in a way. They need something from me. I feel this without anybody telling me. If it doesn't work out, I'll resort to your idea. We'll help them get established then. It'll be a fall back plan."

"Delilah, I swear to Christ I'm not trying to talk you out of this. This is what I do for you, and you know that. I identify options. But when people move into your home, it always takes a stick of fucking dynamite to get them out."

"These aren't those people, Dobro. They're so different."

"How about we split the difference?" said Dobro Temple. "How about you take one of them in? Maybe the girl. Maybe you take in the girl, and you let me take care of getting the guy set up someplace. How would that be? Does he have any skills?"

"I want to think he's pretty good at praying. But I have to tell you, Dobro, that after a couple of nights ago, the two of them might be a package deal."

"What do you mean?" he asked.

"A couple nights ago, they did the deed. It was the priest's first time."

Dobro nodded his head and sighed into the phone. He flipped his pad of paper to a new page. He looked at his watch and knew that he was several minutes late for a call with a guy looking for help getting a television show about circus freaks out of preliminary development. He smiled and thought himself the luckiest bastard on the planet. Who wouldn't want this life? Dealing with circus freaks and crippled, old, fat rock stars looking to adopt fellow patients from a mental hospital. Who wouldn't sign on for this package?

"Okay, baby," he said, "what do you need from me?"

Meryl

Millie Chase was one of Meryl's better clients. She showed up early, but not too early, and she visited The Garden of Healing almost every Tuesday afternoon.

Millie enjoyed spending an hour each week with her. She found Meryl to be a kind-hearted, if kooky, woman. Occasionally, Meryl would ask a question or suggest a subject matter for discussion that Millie knew was right out of Counseling 101, but for the most part the sessions were free-wheeling and comfortable.

"How was your week?"

This was the standard opening from Meryl as each woman assumed their same positions in the converted living room. On this day, a chilly and breezy afternoon that reminded Millie a bit of living on the shores of Lake Ontario, Millie had much to tell.

"I started my classes. I'm taking two this semester, just to get back in the swing of things. I figure I can knock out the degree sometime next year. I'm still fighting with them about a couple of classes not transferring."

"I hate it when they do that," said Meryl. "When I decided to get my Masters, they almost didn't give me credit for a course I took *there*. At their own school, even."

Meryl wore a flowing dress made of stone-washed denim that fell to her calf and buttoned at her neck. Red, high-top basketball sneakers and white knee socks completed the ensemble. A strand of pearls lay around her neck. She held a blue crystal in her lap as the two of them chatted.

"How are things at home?" she asked Millie. "You guys still having positive conversation?"

Millie nodded.

"For the most part," she said. "Listen, I have no idea how all-consuming Edward's job can be. I mean, I watched him through med school and residency and all of that. I saw the strain it put on him. And I kind of hoped that once he got out in the world, once he was working in his field instead of just learning how to work in his field, that it might be easier on him."

"But I hasn't been?" asked Meryl.

"Not easier. Just different, I guess. He tries so hard not to bring it home. But that's almost impossible."

"What does he bring home?"

Millie shifted in her easy chair. She tucked her left leg under her and picked up a crystal. On this occasion she went with red. She had removed her ankle boots and was sock-footed.

"I probably shouldn't tell you this, but he talks quite a bit about his patients at the hospital. I'm pretty sure he isn't supposed to be doing that, but he needs some sort of release, doesn't he? I mean, a lot of shrinks…he hates it when I call them that, it's okay when he does, but not when I do…a lot of them see therapists themselves. Just to maintain their equilibrium, you know. He's decided against that. So, he has me."

"Does this bother you, Millie? How does this make you feel? What color does this make you feel?"

Millie smiled at this. She knew that she would share this last question with her husband when he got in that evening. What color does this make me feel?

Millie held up the red crystal and inspected it for flaws.

"I feel bad, but I almost derive a guilty pleasure from some of the shit he tells me. I'm not supposed to be hearing some of the things these crazy people do and say, but some of it is really funny."

Meryl caressed the crystal in her lap. She had embraced the holistic approach to healing that she now practiced at The Garden. Aromas, crystals, musical tones, sand, all of these were her tools of the trade. And she understood that the husband of the client sitting now across the coffee table from her attempted to heal his patients in an entirely different way. There was counseling to be sure, but drugs were a big part of the package in modern-day psychiatry, and Meryl knew this. She also strongly suspected that neither of them used the word *crazy* when discussing their patients.

"Crazy might be a bit of a harsh word to use, Millie. What do you think?"

Millie smiled.

"That's what Edward would say."

"There are actually a couple different theories as to why he cut his ear. And, no, he didn't cut the entire ear off."

This was David Bouchard lecturing in a classroom fitted with thirty seats but occupied by only nine students. This was the upper level class *Van Gogh and the Post-Impressionist Period*. Millie Chase had taken a version of this class several years ago while studying in Elmira, New York, but the credit had not transferred to Weatherly.

David Bouchard had earned a PhD from The University of Virginia in Charlottesville, had joined the faculty at Weatherly as an Instructor, and had in the last two years risen to the position of Associate Professor. He was a man most accurately described as one possessing no pretentiousness. He was handsome in an art professor kind of way. His blonde hair was long and tied into a ponytail; he had a mustache that he failed, on a relatively frequent basis, to keep trimmed. His body was that of a swimmer; his hands were often red and chapped, even in warmer months. To a person, the students and fellow-faculty members at Weatherly thought he was gay.

"The first theory is that he was cut in a bit of a tussle with a fellow artist. He was well known for many unhealthy traits, among them drinking too much and projecting anti-social behavior. This theory is the one I tend to lean towards.

The second one, and it's gained a lot of traction in today's world of psychoanalyzing everything, is that he cut it himself in an effort to quiet the voices he claimed to be hearing. I'm not learned enough in the field of psychology to make a judgement call on that. He pretty clearly suffered from some serious mental illnesses, but let's not get bogged down by that. Let's talk about how he went from being a rather pedestrian maker of pictures to the artist we celebrate today. Let's talk about Arles."

Millie liked David Bouchard. She liked that he could not be easily described, that he possessed many individual qualities that differentiated him from many other types of men. He spoke of trips he'd taken to The Netherlands, to Spain, to Italy to visit the museums containing the works of many great masters. He talked of playing the cello from the age of four. He had a photo of his dog, some sort of smallish mutt, on one of the shelves of a bookcase in his tiny office on campus. He was not, in Millie's eyes, analytical. He appeared to allow life to flow over him. He wore non-descript slacks and a tweed jacket almost every day.

Millie was older than all of the students in the two classes she was taking at Weatherly, but this did not bother her. She was still young and possessed of a physical beauty that lit up a room when she would enter. The Asian features, the long legs, the spark that seemed always to appear in her eyes when she smiled.

"This is very good work, Millie," said David Bouchard.

They were seated in the cramped space of his tiny office. There was barely enough room for a bookshelf, a desk and David's chair, let alone two other chairs for visitors, but David had felt it important to review his students' work in person. He made office time available for each and every one of them.

"It's unusual for me to read a paper that not only contains the background that we've reviewed in class, but also adds in new information like you did. I can tell that you've done more research on your own, and I appreciate it."

He could have left his remarks at simply praising the effort, but Millie was warmed by the fact that he had expressed appreciation. He was certainly a different kind of man from those she had been around. For the most part, she guessed that he was seemingly assured of himself and not needing confirmation from those around him. He seemed not to possess an agenda of any kind. His feelings were worn on the sleeve of his tweed jacket.

"Thanks," she said. "You know, I took this class before. When I was in school in New York State I took a class just like this one. I think the name of the course was even the same. So, I've had a bit of an edge on my classmates. Maybe I took some of what I put into this paper from some subconscious well of information from the previous class, you know?"

"You're too special to be humble," said David Bouchard. "Keep up the good work, Millie."

She rose from her chair and turned towards the doorway. The door had remained open throughout their conversation. The space was no less confining.

Before leaving the office, she turned back to the professor.

"Thank you for taking the time to review my paper," she said. "I'm not used to that. I've not had other professors willing to do that, and I want you to know it's appreciated."

Then, the result of an urge she felt but had no idea why, she extended her hand. She had a marginally firmer grip than did Dr. Bouchard, but she suspected that he might have been being careful.

"This is delicious," said Edward as he dug into the beef stew Millie had prepared for their dinner. His day had been long and arduous. Representatives from the State Commission on Mental Health had visited the hospital for a day-long review of the facilities and its processes. At the end of the day, shortly after seven PM, the visitors piled into their state-owned sedan and headed back to Richmond.

"What did your visitors say? Do you pass muster?" asked Millie.

She was standing at the counter in the kitchen as she ate her soup in small spoonfuls. She had waited for him so that they could eat dinner together.

"Mil, why do you never sit down when you eat? I swear, the only time you and I are at eye level is when we're eating in a restaurant someplace."

"It's a position of dominance," she said without looking at him. "It makes me feel superior."

Edward kept his head down as he spooned large bites of stew.

"I haven't eaten a thing all day," he said.

"Don't they break for lunch? Are they robots?"

He smiled at this. Millie was closer to the truth than she could have imagined. The visitors, a young woman with multiple degrees in Social Science and bad skin, and an older man whose outdatedness in the field of mental health was surpassed only by his arrogance at being a representative on the governor's pet project committee, displayed nothing close to resembling personality.

"I think they are. You're probably right on that, Mil."

"Why do you deal with them? Why don't you have one of the other doctors walk them around? And why didn't you eat lunch?"

"Funding. That's the answer to your first question. They need to see my face so that they can report back to their committee that all is well, that all of us at the hospital are properly engaged. And I didn't have time for lunch. We processed a couple of patients out this afternoon and I had to see them...wanted to see them individually before they left."

"Who left? If you can say."

Edward raised a finger as he chewed and swallowed a large bite of stew.

"This is so good," he said. "Remember the rock star? Delilah Duncan? Remember her?"

"Sure. I thought she already left."

"She checked out about a week ago. But she developed friendships with my priest and my Latin American woman. I'm not sure if I mentioned that they were both suicide attempts, by the way. Anyway, we released those two this afternoon. We were holding them on court orders, each of them, but it would have been difficult to keep them longer then their thirty days."

"You can cure them in thirty days? They're both good now?" said Millie.

"As good as we can get them in a month," said Edward. "I've seen some positives from each of them. We've kind of done what we can at this point. Anyway, the two of them are moving in with this Delilah Duncan. She apparently has a huge house somewhere in the area, and she asked them to move in with her."

"How do you feel about that? Is that going to work?"

"It frightens the hell out of me, to be honest. It's great that they all became buddies. That's a huge development, believe me. But this triangle of interdependence might be really problematic. There's not a hell of a lot I can do about it, though."

Edward rose and walked to the stove for more stew. He stopped to kiss his wife on the neck, clearing her black hair away with his free hand.

"How's school?" he asked as he took his seat at the table.

"Good. I like both classes, especially the one on Van Gogh. I think you'd like it. All the psychological stuff. The mental health angle. The schizophrenia. Right up your alley, Edward."

"That's just what we need. Some art professor who maybe took a freshman level class in psychology sharing his insights on mental health. I bet he can't even spell schizophrenia."

Millie turned away from the counter. She rinsed her bowl in the sink and placed it in the dishwasher.

"I'm glad your visit with the state people went well today," she said. "I'm going to read for a bit."

Edward sat and finished his stew. His hunger alleviated, he climbed the stairs for a shower and some comfortable clothes.

"I've lived in some very nice places," said Nuncia, "but this one takes the cakes."

She was taking the tour of Delilah Duncan's rather expansive home, a massive, five thousand square foot ranch on top of a hill overlooking horse farms. The drive up to the place from the main road, Nuncia and Dud riding in the second row of seats in the hospital's mini-van, had seemed to take forever. Delilah was standing in her crutches at the front door waiting for them. Once welcomed, they were given a guided tour by the keeper-of-the-house. Jon had been with Delilah for several years. He slept in a small bedroom off of the kitchen and attended to every detail. His level of attentiveness to Delilah's needs was unwavering. And he had learned, on just about the first day of employment, that his was not an opinion that mattered if it differed from hers.

"Just tell him he's fired and to get the fuck out of your house," Dobro had told her on the phone. "I'm not crazy about the guy, anyway."

Jon was subordinate from that day forward, but only just.

"This will be your room, Nuncia," he said as he and his two new housemates entered the *blue room*. "The Blue Room, I like to call it. Full bathroom there," he said pointing.

Nuncia tossed her knapsack onto the twin-size bed. Even living at Jawan's mansion in Miami had not been this nice. It was not so much that Delilah's house was any larger or any more elaborate. It had furniture. And furniture can go a long way towards making a place homey.

"Where are you sleeping, Dud?" she asked

"This way, please," said Jon.

And then to Nunica: "and please let me know if there is any little thing we can do to make your stay here with us more enjoyable."

These words left his mouth with the aroma of sulfur. All three of them picked up on the scent, but only Dud seemed even the slightest bit put off.

Nuncia and John Dudley settled into separate routines that seemed to almost never intersect. They both were aware of the importance of staying busy, and each of them offered to help around the house. Jon was reluctant to provide them with even the slightest task. The more his two new housemates became ingrained in the day-to-day fabric of life at Delilah's, the longer these intrusions into his world were likely to last. In the end, it was always Delilah who ruled the moment.

"Jesus Christ, Jon, let them go get the groceries. It's one turn out of the driveway, for heavens sakes. They're not going to get lost. They can take the truck."

Delilah owned two vehicles, but the black full-size SUV with big wheels and a loud and powerful motor seemed the one to fit her personality the least. It could have been used to transport the governor, or maybe The Secretary of State. The other was a Mercedes four door sedan. Jon hated it when anyone other than himself drove either of them.

"One of you knows how to drive, right?" Delilah asked.

"I do," said Nuncia.

"As do I," offered Dud as an afterthought.

Jon handed the keys to Nuncia as if they were made of blown glass.

"Please be careful," he said.

"Lighten the fuck up, Jon," said Delilah.

Nuncia was only just a touch over five feet tall, and the climb up into the giant SUV was a challenge.

"I feel like I'm climbing into a rocket ship," she said to Dud.

"Just be careful," he said. "You wouldn't want to disappoint Jon, would you?"

"Jon can kiss my butt," she said as she started the motor. "Do you have the list?"

"I do. Do we have any money?"

Nuncia opened her door and hopped down. Dud sat in the SUV as she entered the house and, after thirty seconds, re-emerged.

"God, we are pathetic," she said climbing back up into the vehicle. "Thank God you thought about how we're supposed to pay for all of this. Delilah gave me a credit card. That would have been horrible."

"Do you want me to drive on the way back?" asked Dud.

"You can push the cart in the store," Nuncia answered.

On warmer days when the paved driveway from Delilah's house down to the main road was dry, the three former patients at Botetourt State Hospital hiked to the bottom and back. The round trip was just short of a mile, and they enjoyed the fresh air, the scenic beauty of the adjacent horse farms and the exercise. Delilah owned a motorized wheelchair which she almost never used. As a portion of the driveway was rather steep, she commanded that both Dud and Nuncia hold on as she rolled slowly down the drive.

"This will be a good way to kill me if it comes to that," she said as they inched along over the steepest section. "Just wheel my fat ass out here and let me go. It'll be like a bobsled run at the Olympics, only I'll probably break my bloody neck when I crash."

At the bottom of the hill, mail was collected out of the box beside the road and placed in Delilah's lap for the arduous trip back up the slope. She wore sunglasses and didn't seem the least concerned that her two drivers were having to exert so much energy on the return trip. The motor driving her chair was no match for the grade of the hill.

"Heave Ho, my hearties," she said. "Keep it up. We're almost home."

Two nights per week, Nuncia made dinner. She had asked Jon on numerous occasions if she could help Martha, the woman who cooked lunch and dinner every day at Delilah's before heading home to her husband, a bearded man who worked the night shift at a truck stop convenience store.

Jon made it a point to be gone on these occasions. Martha was an adequate cook who prepared marginally nutritious meals which leaned heavily towards carbs. It was more important to her that her diners leave the table sated rather than enamored of the flavors they had just enjoyed. Jon didn't so much like her cooking, as much as he resented Nuncia's intrusion into the kitchen.

"This is how I tried to kill myself," she said one late afternoon as she was doing the prep work necessary for that evening's meal.

Delilah was sitting at the table in the kitchen, a large glass of red wine resting within inches of her right hand. Nuncia noticed the lack of the circular movement that seemed less and less an affliction but did not comment on it.

"Cutting up vegetables? You tried to kill yourself by cutting up vegetables?"

"A fish. A very dangerous and poisonous fish. It's called fugu fish. People in Japan eat it, but milder fugu fish are here in America as well. I got one through the restaurant. A guy who sold me all my meats and fish, he got me one. I told him I was just going to inspect it, that maybe I'd be opening an Asian restaurant and that I wanted to just look at it, cut it open a little. I was curious, that's what I told him. But I ate some."

"Is that the fish where the chefs have to study for a long time..."

"Eight years," interrupted Nuncia, "they study for eight years before they're allowed to cook this fish for any customers. I studied for about eight minutes."

"Why the fish?" asked Delilah as she sipped her wine. "God, this is really good. So nice and light and still big enough for flavor. What is it?"

"It's a pinot noir. Dud and I got it at that little market, not at the big grocery store."

"Get some more next time, will you? It's very good. So, back to the fish. Why the fish?"

"When I found out that my little sister Claudia was forced by those bad men to drink bleach, I couldn't stand it. I couldn't stand to be alive and to be feeling all this life running through my veins. All I could think about was my little sister being raped and abused by these men, only because my father had bought alcohol with the little bit of money that they told him to give them. She was punished because of what my father did and because I was not able to send money to keep her protected. I didn't want to live if Claudia could not."

Nuncia said all of this in a matter-of-fact voice. She did not look away from the knife and her vegetables the entire time she spoke.

"Was it awful?" asked Delilah. "When you eat the fish, is it awful?"

"I wanted to eat it because that's the way Claudia felt when she drank that bleach. When you eat the fish...the fugu...your lips and mouth go numb, then your stomach feels like there is a fire in there. In a few minutes, you have a hard time breathing. Then you die."

"Why didn't you die?"

"The fish wasn't strong enough. It just made me very sick. I was in the hospital for several days. They had to hook me up to a breathing machine. I don't know why I told them that I had done this on purpose. But then I wouldn't have been sent to the crazy-person hospital. I wouldn't have met you or Father Dud."

"Geesh," said Delilah. "The things we learn about people in the kitchen, right?"

Nuncia stepped away from the cutting board on the counter and delivered the opened bottle of pinot noir to Delilah. She filled her glass as if serving a high-end client in her restaurant, a slight twist of the bottle at the end. She noted once again the lack of circular motion as Delilah's right arm and hand rested on the table.

Nuncia resumed chopping and Delilah looked out the window. Warmer months were clearly on the horizon, but it was still early enough in the year for the sky to darken in the late afternoon. Delilah enjoyed the days when Nuncia cooked. She always enjoyed the food prepared by Martha, but Nuncia's skill level was vastly superior. Nuncia built flavors and the food was healthier. And Delilah enjoyed sitting in the kitchen as Nuncia worked. She had serious knife skills that Delilah marveled at.

"What are you making?" Delilah asked.

Nuncia smiled widely without looking away from her cutting board.

"Fish," she said. "But don't worry. I'm grilling a grouper, not trying to kill us."

"Would it ruin your outing if I decided to pass on going with you?"

"Not at all, Edward. I told you all along that you didn't have to go. It's a local art showing, probably not very good. And I'll only be gone for an hour or two."

Millie was seated at a small vanity in their bedroom. She elected to apply make-up only on special and more formal occasions, and always very lightly. She brushed her black hair and opted for lip balm instead of the tube of coral lipstick she had been considering.

"If you're sure, then I've got some stuff I need to review for work. Maybe when you get back, we can talk about going out for dinner."

"Whatever works for you, Edward. I won't be long."

As she drove towards campus Millie wondered if her husband's reluctance to attend the art show was truly derived from a workload that needed his attention or if some other factor was playing a part. Granted, she was well aware that the quality of what she was about to enjoy was, at best, small-college interpretive expression. But she also knew that there was a basketball game on television that afternoon that Edward had expressed some interest in watching. It didn't bother her.

Attending the art show had been Professor Bouchard's idea. He had tossed it out as a suggestion to his class that week.

"Listen, let's not delude ourselves into thinking we're going to be in the presence of greatness. That being said, I will say that I've seen a lot of the work that's going to be on display, and some of it is actually pretty good. But let's remember that these are young people not any older than you."

He looked at Millie as he delivered this last statement. She detected a smile, but a very slight one.

"I think that if you can attend, even if it's for an hour, you might enjoy it. As I said, some of the work is pretty good. And it will be a good exercise for us to try to find similarities between what we see on the walls and what we look at in class. Everybody gets influenced by some thing or someone. Maybe it would be good to play detective and see if we can make any connections. Keep a notebook if you'd like and we can talk about it next week."

Attendance at the art showing was purely optional, but Millie decided to go as soon as she learned about it. Among her other reasons, Professor Bouchard had pointed out that the students whose work was on the walls would benefit from the support.

"The more, the better," he had said.

"Hello, Millie," said Professor Bouchard. "I'm so glad you could come this afternoon. It means so much to these students to have a full house."

"I think your idea to look for influences…to see if any of the big boys can be seen as influencing what these students are doing, is a great one. I've kind of liked doing that."

"I won't ask you to share your insights, unless, of course, you would like to," he said.

He was wearing a pair of jeans, and this was the first time Millie had seen him in anything other than dark slacks. The low collared shirt and tweed sport coat, Professor Bouchard's uniform, had been replaced by a sweater. Something Norwegian would have been Millie's guess.

"No. I'll show some," she said. "Back here. I'll share a couple I thought of."

"No fare going with the Jackson Pollock," he said.

Millie Chase was at least three inches taller than the professor, but this bothered neither of them

"My husband always says that if it's something he can do, then it's not art," she said.

Millie and Professor Bouchard had taken seats in the student lounge adjacent to the hall where the hopes and aspirations of dozens of art students from a multiplicity of genres hung on the walls. They had carried clear plastic cups of lower-end chardonnay from the bar set up near the doorway connecting the two rooms. Professor Bouchard had offered to pay the two dollars for Millie's wine, but she had politely declined.

"Not a bad definition, actually," he said. "There's merit to that."

"There's merit to everything Edward says and does, Professor Bouchard. You have no idea."

"David. Please."

Millie smiled.

"I remember when I was in school before, in New York State, some of the teachers used to almost demand the students refer to them by their first names only. It was funny. It's like they were so intent upon being hip, and that was the clearest way to be taken that way. Is that you, David? Wanting me to use your first name so that you can be hip?"

"Guilty as charged. So, what did you think of the work we saw today?"

Millie recrossed her legs. She noticed that her professor did not look away from her eyes as she did this.

"Fully aware of the fact that I have so little talent as far as being able to produce anything myself, I have to say that I wasn't overwhelmed with any of the work I saw. I'm just being honest because you asked, but it felt more like a high school art show than what I'd expect from college kids. Sorry if that is insensitive or if it offends you. When I was at Delacroix that summer…I went after my senior year in high school for a month-long program…the stuff I saw those kids doing was phenomenal. Believe me, it reoriented my whole thinking. I knew good and damn well right then that I was never going to be an artist in the sense of painting or anything like that. I wasn't in that same league."

"We have to be honest if we're going to be critical of what we see. And I use that word as in *art critics*, not critical in a pejorative sense. If we don't call 'em like we see 'em, we're frauds. And, trust me, we don't get to be tenured if we're frauds. At least not in the art department."

Millie finished her plastic cup of wine and stood to leave.

"David, it has been a pleasure walking around with you. And I want to thank you for not being all pedantic and know-it-all with the artwork. It was way more fun than I anticipated having this afternoon. But I have to be going."

"I'm right there with you, Millie. Keep this to yourself, but I feel like I've done my good deed for the day, coming here. Team player in the department and all of that. Come on. I'll walk out with you."

They deposited their empty cups in a recycling container next to the bar and moved towards the doorway leading out to the parking area. Millie accepted his offer to see her to her car.

"What's your husband do?" he asked, "some sort of doctor, right?"

"Psychiatrist," she said.

"That's more years of school than I want to think about," said David. "I'm dying of curiosity to see what the wife of a psychiatrist drives."

"It's always all about cars with boys, isn't it?"

They arrived at Millie's parking place, and he opened the door for her after she had unlocked it.

"Pretty practical," he said. "I'm surprised. A Honda. I would have guessed Mercedes."

"My husband drives a big BMW, and my parents each drive a Mercedes. Edward is always trying to get me to get a new car. He offers to buy me one on a monthly basis. But I'm good with this. I've had it since college."

"Well, drive safely," he said. "See you in class."

Millie smiled as she thought of seeing Professor Bouchard standing in front of his students the following week. His ponytail would be positioned perfectly; his tweed jacket would be restored to its revered position as the anchor to his this-is-how-we-look-in-academia wardrobe.

She placed a hand on each of his shoulders, bent down slightly and, rather quickly, kissed him. Her lips were parted, her tongue brushing up against his closed mouth.

"I have no earthly idea why I just did that," she said. "I'm really sorry."

She was smiling as if she'd just been caught stealing a cookie. It did not bother her for a moment that he was silent.

As she slid into her seat behind the steering wheel, he stood and held the frame of her car door. She was shaking her head and continued smiling.

"You're going to get me in trouble, Millie. You're a bad influence on me. I can feel it."

"I've never been a bad influence on anybody," said Millie.

She was seated in her usual position at The Garden of Healing and had just shared the art show episode with Meryl. She wore black yoga pants and a hooded sweater. On this day, she wore running shoes. They were, as always, left at the door. Her yellow ankle socks had toes. Meryl commented on them more than once.

"And I truly can't recall doing anything bad before, even as a girl. My family is very old-school Korean. We don't do things like kiss strange men."

"Apparently, you're the one to break the mold. And don't beat yourself up for this. You got caught off guard a little bit. You kind of got caught up in the moment and had a little hiccup."

"I don't know if it's such a little hiccup. I've replayed the moment a lot in my mind. It's going to be weird seeing Professor Bouchard in class tomorrow, but I'm kind of excited about it. Is that crazy?"

Meryl took a cleansing breath. The crystal on her lap this day was green.

"This is what I know, Millie: we humans are all blessed with a full spectrum of sexuality. We like and dislike such a variety of things, and those likes and dislikes change over time. I used to like biker guys. Big guys with lots of tattoos and leather pants and all of that. They almost repulse me now. Our sexual preferences just change, that's all."

Millie shook her head.

"This isn't about sex, believe me. Edward and I have a terrific sex life. We do it several times a week, and it's extremely fulfilling. I used to kid him that the reason he's so good at oral sex is all those anatomy classes he had to take in med school. No guesswork for my husband. And I don't believe I'm talking so openly about this."

"Well," said Meryl, "that's always a good sign. You know, you've spoken about how Edward's schedule can be pretty all-consuming, about how he brings his work home quite often. And you shared that this weekend, he elected to stay home and watch a game on television instead of going to the art exhibit with you. Maybe your episode was just a reaction of how you felt about that. How you're feeling about that."

"Maybe. There might be something to that," said Millie.

"So, what are you going to do about your professor?"

"My plan is to apologize to him and to put it behind me. If he would prefer I leave the class, I'll do that. He could get in serious trouble, and none of it is any of his fault."

"You know me, I don't often make suggestions. My style is to try to get stuff out on the table and have my clients determine what's a good plan, or what's not so good. But in this case, I just want to tell you that you might be making more of this than it warrants. You kissed a guy. Once. Is it so terribly different from shaking someone's hand? I mean, when we meet someone who is interesting or even attractive to us, isn't it a tiny bit physical…even sexual…when we shake hands with them?"

"You're probably right. I'm going to try and let it all slide away. Not fret about it so much. That's helpful, Meryl. It truly is."

"And it's okay to have thoughts about this professor. We're all human, Millie."

Millie stretched her long legs out in front of her. They were bare from the ankle to mid-calf. She nodded again as she selected a crystal, red, and placed it in her lap.

"To your point about the whole spectrum of what attracts us and what doesn't, David is not in the ballpark with Edward. Edward is a big guy. And he's very attentive and patient sexually. David is a good three inches shorter than me."

"It takes all kinds, right? I can't wait to hear about it next week. You know, if something comes up where you want to meet sooner, just give me a call."

"Thanks again, Meryl. It's such a relief to have someone to tell all of this to."

"I just love those socks," said Meryl. "I would look goofy in those things, but you really make them work."

Meryl walked Millie to the door and waited for her to put her shoes on. She watched Millie through a window in the foyer as the younger woman walked to her car, got in and drove away.

Meryl locked the door. Her next session was not for an hour. A couple in their mid-fifties who were making one last attempt at counseling before pulling the plug on a marriage that had probably never pleased either of them.

Meryl walked to the sofa she had just been sitting on. She slipped off her clogs and then the loose-fitting burgundy dress she was wearing. She pulled each arm out of its bra strap and unclasped the back after having twisted it around to her front.

She lay on the sofa and covered herself with the orange and brown blanket she had purchased years ago at a Native American gift shop in New Mexico. The room was still and was lighted only by the candles she had not blown out. Meryl closed her eyes and breathed rhythmically, slow at first, more rapidly as she allowed herself to replay the conversation she had just had with Millie. The images that raced through her mind were of Millie and Edward having sex, of the professor kissing Millie, of Millie's socks, her toes individually snuggled in yellow.

Dobro

"Go back," said Delilah. "Go back to that station. The one with the preacher guy."

She, Nuncia and Dud were on their way back to the mansion after an outing at the bowling alley. Nuncia drove the big SUV as Delilah navigated from the front seat passenger side. John Dudley sat in the middle of the back seat; his arms stretched out on the head rests to each side of him. The center seatbelt barely reached around his waist.

It had been Nuncia's idea to go bowling. Weekends were typical of all other days for the three of them, with the exception that these were Martha's days off. Nuncia and Dud usually shopped on Saturday morning for items to prepare for Saturday and Sunday dinners. She cooked; he tended to the housekeeping tasks he was comfortable tackling: sweeping, running the vacuum, dusting furniture. Jon, the self-proclaimed manager of the house, was pleasantly absent most weekends. Where he went to hide, none of them knew or cared about.

But this Saturday they had decided to shake things up and revisit the bowling alley where Peter had ordered a drink and where the guard had to be called in to shut him up.

Delilah sat at the plastic table and pretended to keep score. She knew less about bowling than probably anyone in the building, but her crutches, leaning against the unoccupied seat next to her, gave her a certain gravitas that no one else in the place possessed. She looked the part. Professional-bowler-laid-low-by-enigmatic-neurological-disorder-but-wanting-to-stay-in-the-sport kind of thing.

"I love those preachers on AM radio," said Delilah. "I count the seconds I can stand them until they ask for money. It's never over a minute."

On cue the man delivering salvation and admonishment in equal doses beseeched his listeners to help keep his program on the air by sending in what they could afford.

"Jesus will thank you if you help us keep His message on the airwaves," said the man. "And He will not think too kindly on any of you who don't."

"Enough," said Delilah. "God, but those fuckers are all the same. People call in with real problems and all they get back is advice to pray harder and send in more money. God knows how many people these guys could really be helping if they just went off script once in their lives."

Nuncia searched for a new station, her eyes never leaving the road in front of her.

"Why never any FM?" she asked Delilah.

"I don't want to bump into myself on any oldies station. That happened a couple of times. It messed with me. For some reason, it really messed me up."

They drove in silence, the only voices coming from a call-in show featuring listeners intent on selling and buying used household items. Nuncia asked the same question as each item was introduced.

"Who would want that crap?"

As they pulled up to the mansion, Delilah, with not an insignificant amount of effort, turned halfway around so as to look at John Dudley.

"You should do that," she said.

"Do what?"

"You should do a radio show. Like the preacher guy, but only civilized. You could listen to people's problems and give them advice, not just accuse them of being sinful. You know your bible…that's a big part of why these poor bastards call in. They want to know that the Lord is on their side, is looking out for them."

Dud felt his ears reddening. This was a sensation he had not had in weeks.

"I wouldn't have the foggiest notion of what to say. God, I might do more damage than good."

"That's not true," said Nuncia. "Look what you did for that boy Peter, Dud. You talked to him, and he actually got a little better. You probably saved him, Dud. You'd know what to say on a radio show."

Delilah opened her car door and began the tedious task of climbing down from the big SUV.

"Think about it, Father," she said. "It might be what the Lord put you here to do."

"I'll tell you one thing," said the former priest, "if I ever did anything like this, the last thing I would do would be to hide behind God. That's bullshit."

"Just think about it, Dud," said Nuncia as she climbed down out of the vehicle. "You'd be great."

"I wouldn't know where to begin," said John Dudley. "I wouldn't have a clue how to get something like that started."

"Just think about it, Dud," said Delilah. "If it's something we want to do, I can handle all the legwork. I know a guy."

The sunny young woman sitting outside Dobro Temple's office answered Delilah's call and transferred it quickly to her boss. She loved the part of her job that allowed her to exchange pleasantries with celebrities, but not so much when Delilah Duncan called.

"She used to be the sweetest thing in the world," Dobro explained to her after one particularly clipped conversation, "but she got old, she kind of has some sort of weird disease that affects her motor skills, she's fat. It's a lot to deal with after having been on top of the world. It's not you, trust me."

These images of suffering had touched the young woman's heart. She felt genuine sympathy for Delilah from that day forward. She was polite to a level of saccharine with each call she took from the mansion.

"What's up, sunshine?"

"Dobro, I need a little favor. I need you to make some magic happen."

He placed his feet on his desk and balanced a legal pad on his lap; he had recently replaced the cartridge in his expensive pen. He settled the receiver back into the phone cradle and put Delilah on speaker.

"Talk to me," he said.

"You remember my priest? The guy I met at the loony bin and brought home?"

"Of course, I do. With the girl, right? The chef lady from South America?"

"Central America, actually. Panama. But that's not important."

"I'm listening, Delilah. What are we doing?"

"We were driving back from the bowling alley the other day...can you even believe that? That I went bowling...and we hear this radio show. It's on some Podunk AM station and it's all about this preacher guy railing against Satan and sinners...one of those guys who probably gets off reading about prostitutes getting stoned to death for going against God's will. Anyway, we all start thinking about it, about how Dud used to be a priest and did a shit ton of counseling with people in various tough positions, how he did a really nice thing in helping this boy at the hospital, how he's just kind of good at drawing people out in this low-key, undramatic kind of way."

"I'm listening," said Dobro.

"We want to do a radio show. A call in. One hour a week where people call in with whatever ails them, and Dud offers up advice. Not always spiritual advice, but I see him just talking people off of cliffs, you know?"

Dobro stopped writing and place his pen on his desk.

"OK, first off, there's a real liability issue with your idea, Delilah. It can certainly be worked around with a disclaimer at the beginning of every show...I'll have someone work that up for us...but is your priest strong enough to deal with all the stuff that might be coming his way? What was he in the hospital for?"

"He tried to kill himself. Slit his wrists."

"Jesus, Delilah, you can sure pick 'em."

"I think he'll do fine, Dobro. I'll keep a close eye on him. If it seems to be getting to him too much, I'll just pull the plug on the show."

"Might you want to talk to one of his doctors or something? Just make sure *they* feel good with this idea?"

"Listen," said Delilah, "if that would make you feel better, knock yourself out. The head honcho at the hospital is named Doctor Chase. But you should know from experience that he's not going to tell you one thing. Doctor patient privilege. Thank God for that, actually. Right?"

"For sure," said Dobro. "Okay, I think I can get you going with a few phone calls. Unless you want me to come out and set this stuff up in person."

"You don't need to come out, Dobro, unless you want to. I know you're busy out there in La La Land making all those movie stars rich."

"You don't happen to know the call letters of the radio station, do you, Delilah? That would be helpful."

"No, but the station is somewhere around twelve hundred on the dial."

Dobro Temple made a lot of money. He lived in a small but splendidly decorated house in Topanga Canyon. He loved the income but loved the job more. Part of it was putting his clients in touch with industry big shots, the men and women who made casting decisions for motion pictures and television shows, who signed musicians to record labels, who made the decisions on who could write funny dialogue and who could not. But another element of his role as agent-confidante was in taking care of details. He was well known as the kind of guy who did not shy away from handling things, good and bad, for his clients. He had bailed people out of jail, rescued them from domestic violence, sent them through rehab, helped them bury loved ones. He had, in Delilah's case, freed her from an immoral mother who, if left alone to continue plundering the profits from her daughter's celebrity, would have crushed the young woman's career just as it was getting started. He had, in one instance, arranged for a mail-order bride to be delivered from Minsk in Belarus to a client of his who had opted for a rustic life and bought a large horse ranch in Montana. It even fell to Dobro to select the lucky woman from a catalog. "You know my type," said the actor-now-rancher and soon-to-be husband. "Nothing too worldly." Dobro refused to deal with drugs or hookers for his clients. Beyond those self-imposed restrictions, there was little he had not been willing to do in the name of agent and client relationship building. Setting up a radio show on an AM station somewhere in central Virginia would be a piece of cake.

WGOD, the low power AM radio station operated out of an office in a strip mall on the outskirts of Roanoke, was owned by Reverend Robert "Bruiser" Butterman. A self-proclaimed man of God and part-time used car salesman, Butterman had had the foresight to obtain non-profit status for his fledgling empire. His hustle was to invite listeners to donate their vehicles to his Church of Jesus and All That is Holy as a tax write-off, and then sell them, keeping the profits to continue along his path of doing the Lord's work.

The station consisted of a studio roughly the size of a large bathroom. Two microphones hung from the ceiling, and there was room, just barely, for two chairs and a desk. This is where Bruiser and the other hosts sat and delivered the good word while on the air.

A vintage sound board that controlled audio quality, volume and whether or not each microphone was hot rested on a cardboard table in the room adjacent to the studio. A three line telephone took up a corner of the table and was wired into speakers in both rooms. On good days, a screener would field incoming calls and patch them through to whoever was hosting for on-air give and take. A window that appeared to be purchased from a do-it-yourself home improvement expo provided line of sight from one room to the other. The framework was painted white and would have been a more appropriately placed looking out someone's kitchen window at a swing set in the backyard.

Attached to the two rooms making up the studio of WGOD was The Church of Jesus and All That Is Holy. A glorified conference room, it seated twenty or so; folding chairs supplanted wooden pews, but this would all be history as soon as Bruiser obtained the funding needed to move into a real church. He'd had his eye on a stand-alone tobacco shop a mile from the studio. The Smoke Hut's parking lot was almost always empty, the owner's rusted pick-up truck usually the only vehicle in sight. Bruiser was in the early stages of negotiating with the man.

"I'm not going to try to Jew you down," he had said during his last visit. "I'm trying to do the Lord's work here. He doesn't want anybody to make too big a profit is all."

When Bruiser Butterman answered the phone shortly after returning from his most recent negotiating visit with the owner of The Smoke Hut, he would have had no way of knowing his dream of a real church with genuine wooden pews for people to use was one step closer to reality.

"With whom am I speaking?" asked Dobro Temple.

"The Reverend Bob Butterman. But please feel free to call me Bruiser."

"Bruiser, am I speaking to someone affiliated with the radio station in Roanoke, Virginia, eleven-sixty on the AM band?"

"You are, sir. Owner and operator of WGOD."

"Huh. I would have bet good money that those call sign letters would have been snatched up a long time ago," said Dobro.

The wires carrying each man's voice for a couple thousand miles could not have connected two more diverse people, nor have terminated in two more varying locales. Dobro sat in his well-worn swivel chair, his feet contained in a pair of shoes that set him back seven hundred dollars resting on the desk, a legal pad on his lap, the prized Mont Blanc pen from David Bowie ready for action. His office was adorned with several gold and platinum albums, many of them from Delilah Duncan. Photos of celebrities of all shapes, sizes and artistic genres were scattered throughout. The second-floor office was filled with natural light; palm trees lined the street below.

The Reverend was in the control room of WGOD, sitting at the control panel. The space was cramped, the only window in the room looked into the studio. Pictures of Jesus were thumb-tacked to opposite walls. They faced each other without blinking. A Playboy magazine rested on the edge of the card table. The Reverend had obtained a monthly subscription that was delivered to his apartment. The enemies of God and of goodness were everywhere, and it was important that the men and women in battle against them keep well-informed as to their nefarious tactics. The pictures of naked women were not, to Bruiser Butterman, pornography. They were research.

Bruiser had come to find the Lord while serving a three year prison term for writing bad checks. He leaned towards black clothing and wore ankle-high dress boots that zipped up the side. His hair was often slicked back, and his sideburns could have been sliced from squirrel pelts. He lived alone but saw the sixteen year-old daughter of one of the members of his congregation just about every Friday night.

"Bruiser, my name is Dobro Temple. I'm calling from Los Angeles and I have an idea to run by you."

"Dobro," said The Reverend, "now that's not a name you hear every day, is it?"

"It is not. I'm the only Dobro I've ever heard of and, trust me on this Bruiser, in my line of work, you bump into all sorts of interesting names."

"What do you do, Dobro?"

"I represent people. Mostly in the arts, but some business people as well. That's why I'm calling you."

"I'm all ears," said The Reverend.

"I have a client who is interested in sponsoring a call in show on your station. Maybe Friday afternoons for an hour each week."

Bruiser Butterman opened the Playboy to the fold-out section displaying the Playmate of the Month in all of her God-given glory.

"You understand that this is a Christian radio station," he said into the phone. "All of our programming is intended to pass along the teachings of Our Lord and Savior Jesus Christ. You understand that, right, Mister Dobro?"

"Just Dobro. Please. And yes, Bruiser, this show that I'm talking to you about will have a very spiritual flavor to it. The concept is that people call in with their problems. Some of the calls will most certainly be faith-based; some may well be a bit more secular. But all of the calls will be treated as important, and all of the callers will be dealt with in a supportive way. What do you think?"

"Is this a show that you're doing in Los Angeles and shipping over to me?"

"No, Bruiser. The talent is local to your location. He'll be doing the show in studio."

Bruiser turned the page of his magazine and marveled at the perfection of the woman's breasts.

"When you say *secular*, what is it exactly that you're telling me?"

Dobro sat up in his chair, his expensive shoes now resting on the floor beneath him.

"I mean that not everything discussed on the program will be about religion. You have my word that everything will be above board. We certainly have no intention of tarnishing the reputation WGOD has throughout your community. But the show may deal with a wider variety of subject matter than your station currently has running."

"I get most of my programming from a service out of Kansas City, and it costs me plenty," said The Reverend. "Believe me, Dobro, the more local programming I can get, the better. I'm just not sure I want to risk putting someone on the air who could mess up our image...our brand, to use a term I'm sure you big boys out there in California can understand."

Dobro looked at his legal pad. He had, to this point in the conversation, taken no notes.

"The guy doing the show, the talent, has had a ton of theological training, Bruiser. He went to seminary and was a practicing priest for many years before recently going into semi-retirement. Let's be honest here. He's not going to hurt your brand."

"A priest. A Catholic priest, did you say?"

"That's my understanding," said Dobro, a hint of curtness now infusing his voice.

"I'm not sure we need some priest…some Catholic on our airwaves, Dobro. We try really hard to keep the message consistent. We're one hundred present anti-abortion, one hundred percent second amendment, one hundred percent that there's only one way to salvation, and that's through understanding and knowing Jesus. I'm not sure a priest fits in with all of that. We're all about family values here, Dobro."

"Listen," said Dobro, the pleasantness now gone from his tone, "there's a reason my client asked me to reach out to your station, right? She must feel like the show she wants to sponsor would be a good fit with your format. Family values, teachings of Christ, and all of that. She's willing to pay you a thousand bucks a week for the one hour time slot on Fridays from two until three. That comes with someone to run the board and a call-screener. The priest is a very up-and-up guy. He's very connected to God and all of that. He's not going to harm your brand, Reverend Butterman."

Bruiser noted the change in Dobro's demeanor and that he had now addressed him more formally.

"Can I get back to you?" he asked Dobro.

"You can get back to me in fifteen minutes, Reverend. After that, I'm calling a different station. Just putting my cards on the table for you. Stay on the line for a minute. Angelica will give you a number to get right in when you call."

Ten minutes later, after The Reverend Robert "Bruiser" Butterman had called back and accepted the terms previously discussed, he again admired the quality of photography contained in his magazine. He wondered if the woman who worked for Dobro Temple, all the way out there in sunny California, might in some way or another resemble any of the models gracing the pages of his research.

"There's a local attorney I've reached out to. Her name is Mary Hart. She's going to be in contact with you and draw up a contract...nothing fancy...for our deal here. My client wants to get started on the show as quickly as possible. Any problem with that, Bruiser?"

The gentility had returned to Dobro's voice, and the Reverend noticed it.

"No problem at all, Dobro. Listen, let me ask you, what does that Angelica look like? She sounds like a doll baby on the phone."

"She looks just like she sounds. Good doing business with you, Reverend. Call me if something comes up."

"I sure will, Dobro. Hey, maybe some time, if I'm out in California some time, maybe we could get together and grab lunch or something."

"That sounds remarkable," said Dobro in as genuine a voice as he could muster before hanging up the phone.

"Fucking Jew," The Reverend said into the air after hanging up.

John Dudley slept only in fragments the night before his first show.

"However you feel like it's going to be, it's not going to be that bad," Delilah had told him as he announced to his housemates that he was off to bed.

Delilah and Nuncia sat in the expansive living room sipping glasses of white wine and looking at the lights from the houses at the bottom of the hill.

"Just have lots of back-up material," she said. "It's a call-in show, but people might not call in right away. Just go to your back-up stuff, Dud."

"What back-up stuff do you have, Dud?" asked Nuncia.

"Lots, actually. A bible, of course. But I've also got some readings from other religions. Some Buddhist teachings, some poetry from the Sufis."

"Who are the Sufis?" asked Nuncia.

He smiled.

"You'll just have to listen to the show tomorrow to find that out, won't you?"

"Like I have a choice," she shot back.

"Let's remember that we are a Christian radio station," said Bruiser Butterman moments before John Dudley was to go on the air.

After spending the first ten minutes, immediately upon entering the station, in the bathroom, the priest had been given a crash course on how the show was supposed to flow.

"This boy in here," said Bruiser, pointing through the window to the control room, "he'll give you the countdown and tell you when you're on. By law, we have to take some breaks, so I told him to just use station ID stuff as filler. Besides, you'll probably want a break now and then."

"And he screens the calls?"

"Yes, ma'am, he does," he said to Delilah.

He had recognized her as soon as she caned herself into the station, more from her name than her appearance, and was now laying out the ground rules. No faded rock star was going to call the shots in his station.

"We need to make certain that all of the content in this little show of yours meets with our mission."

"What mission is that?" asked Delilah.

"To promote the word of Jesus Christ, of course."

"Well, here's our mission: to promote the idea that someone cares. We want people who might be listening to know that there's someone sitting in this little room here who gives a shit about them. If that's an issue for you, father, then call Dobro. We're just the talent."

"It's not father," said Bruiser, "I'm Reverend Butterman."

"Sorry," said Delilah, "I get you guys mixed up all the time."

No one called. For the first ten minute segment of the show, the phone lines, all three of them, remained empty. Delilah had returned to the big SUV and sat in the front passenger seat listening on the car radio. Dud did his best to keep the dead air to a minimum, but a few minutes into the second segment, there was a solid sixty seconds of silence. He interrupted it with a reading from a Sufi poet, and then gave his listeners a brief account of the origin of Sufiism, but this took up only seconds of airtime.

Then, he was saved. The boy running the control board held up a small chalkboard with the message that there was a caller on hold. John Dudley did as he had been instructed and pressed the blinking light.

"Hello, caller, and welcome to The Hour of Caring."

Dud had gone around and around with Delilah and Nuncia about what to name the show. Nuncia's preference was *The Hour of Power*.

"You know, you could show people that they're in power over their lives, Dud. That would be very good."

Delilah pushed for a more astral, new-age slant.

"Maybe something along the lines of *The New-Age Self-Help Hour*," she said.

In the end, it was Dud's show, and his was the vote that counted.

"Hello," said the caller. "Is this the radio show? Is this The Hour of Caring radio show?"

"Yes, it is. What can I help you with today?"

"I don't know where to start," said the caller. "I'm sorry, but I'm very nervous."

"Please don't be nervous. To be honest, there's probably not a lot of people even listening to us right now. Just talk to me as if we're just talking, okay?"

The caller took a deep breath. Dud sat in the tiny studio and waited.

"I don't know if I believe in God anymore," said the caller.

John Dudley nodded his head and was silent for several seconds.

"Caller, there are so many people who go through periods of questioning the existence of God. You're very much not alone in this. And there is nothing wrong with what you are feeling. Things happen, and intelligent people attempt to make sense of them. It can be very natural for us to have questions. So, may I ask you a few things?"

"Of course," said the caller.

"Okay, is how you're feeling a new thing, or have you been moving in this direction for a while now?"

"It's been with me for a while. Something horrible happened a year ago. I started thinking right then that there could not be a God if this could happen."

"That's common, caller. So, let me ask you this: is your life different since you began to question the existence of God? Are you a different person? Better? Worse?"

There was silence. For a moment, John Dudley feared the caller had hung up.

"I'm improving," said the caller. "When I first started to wonder these things, I was not a good person. I was not happy. I was angry. I'm still angry, but maybe a little bit less."

"Maybe think about this," said Dud. "Maybe think about the possibility that God has been trying to work Himself back into your life since this bad thing happened. Maybe He's sneaking in and that's why you say that you're improving. Do you ever pray, caller?"

"No. I can't pray anymore. It would be like praying to a wall."

"What's wrong with praying to a wall?" asked Dud. "People in Jerusalem pray to a wall all the time. Arabs and Jews. They pray to the same wall."

"You're telling me to pray to a wall?" asked the caller.

"I'm only suggesting that you might try to go through the motions of praying. Whether or not the words you're using are genuine might not be that important. If there is this God who is trying to sneak His way back into your life, maybe He'll hear the words and keep trying to reach you."

"So, I'm not a bad person for feeling the way I do? For wondering if there is a God out there or not?"

"Assuming that there really is a God, do you think He would want to keep trying to be part of your life if you were a bad person? Do you think you would be worth the effort?"

"I suppose you're right," said the caller. "Thank you. I feel a little better. Can I call you again sometime?"

"I'm on the air every Friday from two until three. Call me whenever you want if you think I can help."

As Delilah listened from the comfort of her vehicle, she wondered if Dud was aware of the fact that his first caller had been Nuncia dialing in from the church phone in the room next door. The accent surely had to give her away, but then, who could really know for sure?

The ride back to the mansion was quiet. After initial offerings of congratulations from Nuncia and Delilah, the two women allowed Dud the time to enjoy the silence. Delilah knew from countless experiences performing in front of people that these little respites of nothingness were necessary for recharging of the batteries. She respected Dud's need for space. Nuncia wanted to ask him if he had known all along that she was the first caller but decided against it.

Jon opened the door for Delilah and stepped aside as she caned her way in.

"How was the radio show?" he asked no one in particular.

"You didn't listen?" asked Nuncia. "He was great. He's what you might call *a natural*."

"I'm sure," said Jon in as condescending a voice as he could muster.

"Jon, why don't you fuck off and die," said Nuncia. "And point your nose up at someone else, why don't you? I'm tired of it."

Jon was startled by this level of emotion. His continued existence as Delilah's keeper-of-the-mansion was contingent upon a consistent lack of friction, and he knew this. He knew from past experience that any time Delilah was displeased, a phone call from Dobro Temple would be coming his way. Delilah had no problem laying down the law with Jon; she deferred to Dobro in these matters simply because he was more thorough.

"I am so very sorry," Jon said to Nuncia. "Please believe me that I certainly did not intend to offend anyone."

"I don't believe you for a second," she said as she moved towards the kitchen.

That night, shortly after an exhausted John Dudley had climbed into his bed for what he hoped was going to be a solid night's sleep, there was a light knock on his door. Before he could get up or even respond, Nuncia entered the darkened room and closed the door behind her. The room was dark, the only light coming from a plug-in nightlight under the bedside table and an alarm clock with glowing red numbers.

"I need to talk to you," she said.

He sat up, placing his legs over the side of the bed. Nuncia assumed the same position to his side.

"Delilah asked me to take over running the house just now. She wants to get rid of that shithead Jon, but she needs someone to run things. She wants to keep Martha, but only for a couple days a week. She wants me to do most of the cooking."

"How do you feel about that?" asked the priest.

"I am loving it," said Nuncia. "It's what I was born to do. Take care of a big house. Make sure the people living here get fed with healthy food. And she offered to pay me what she's paying the shithead."

"Will you continue to live here?" he asked. The thought of her leaving, of having her own place to live, was unsettling.

"For as long as she'll have me."

"That's wonderful news, Nuncia. I'm very happy for you."

"Now, get back in bed, Dud."

He resumed his position under the covers and said goodnight.

"Wait a minute," she said.

She stood beside Dud's bed and slowly removed her clothing. During their rendezvous at the State Hospital, the room had been almost entirely dark. This was the first time in John Dudley's life that he had truly been able to lay his eyes on a woman's naked body.

"Scootch over a little," she said before climbing into bed with him. "I want to get on top this time. Do you like that?"

"Nuncia, the only sexual experience I've ever had in my life has been with you. Except for my hand, of course."

"You'll like this, Dud. I promise you will."

When they had finished, when John Dudley had regained his breath and silently wondered at his good fortune, he kissed the top of her head as she nestled into his large body.

"You did a very good thing today," she said. "You're going to do a lot of good with your radio show. You're going to help a lot of people, Dud. This is your reward. For helping all the people you're going to help, this can be your reward."

Dudley again kissed the top of her head.

"I need to tell you one more thing," she said. "That was me on the phone today. Your first caller...it was me from another room."

"I know," he said. "Thank you for saving me."

Millie Chase was far less nervous than she had anticipated being as she climbed the steps to Professor Bouchard's second-floor office. He was sitting at his desk looking out through the doorframe as she neared. His ponytail was tight, his tweed jacket with patches at the elbows hung from the coat stand in the corner.

"Do you have a second, Professor Bouchard?"

He put down the pen he had been using to make notes on the papers he was grading.

"I thought we got past all that, Millie. I thought I was David."

She smiled, but inexpressively.

"Do you have a second, David?"

"Of course. Please, have a seat. I'd offer you coffee or something, but I don't have any."

"I'm fine," she said as she sat. "Listen, I just want to tell you that I'm sorry about what happened in the parking lot. That's very much unlike me, and I really can't explain what came over me. Anyway, I'm sorry and if you want me to leave the class, I'll completely understand."

He held both hands up as if surrendering.

"Whoa, whoa. That's completely not necessary. You're a shining light in this class. You really have to stay and finish it. Hey, stuff happens, like what happened in the parking lot. Let's just put that behind us and focus on the class."

"That's very thoughtful of you, David. Very understanding."

"I've been teaching a long time," he said. "Stuff happens, people get confused. It's okay, Millie."

"Occupational hazard," she said. "Trust me, David, nothing like that will happen again."

He paused and pursed his lips. Millie noticed that his blonde mustache had recently been trimmed.

"It can happen again," he said, "but not on campus. It was a very nice moment, actually. I thought about it all weekend. But you're a married woman, and so I'm not going to do anything that might be inappropriate. I will never pursue you, Millie. But if you ever want to meet me, even if it's just to chat, just let me know."

She stood and extended her hand.

"Let's see what kind of grade you give me," she said as she took his hand rather firmly in her own.

A minute later, as Professor Bouchard was again grading papers, Millie reappeared in the doorway. She entered his tiny office before being invited in and closed the door behind her.

"Does this lock?" she asked.

During the whole episode, removing her shoes, her pants and panties, touching David as he lowered his pants, allowing herself to be bent over his desk and entered from behind, papers flung to the floor, she did the calculations of potential losses: David's job, her own marriage, certainly the education she was endeavoring to complete. Those all could vanish, a result of this one moment. She tried to understand why she was doing this. There was no explanation. It was simply something that she was certain she needed to do.

Tara

Nuncia and Dud each gripped a handle of Delilah's wheelchair as they inched their way to the mailbox at the bottom of the drive. It was a sunny and warming day. The colors of spring were everywhere. Red Bud trees and magnolias painted the hillsides across the valley white and pink.

"Not so fast," said Delilah. "We're not in a race, you two."

Her drivers did not respond but slowed the pace even further as they made their descent. At the bottom, the mail was retrieved and placed in Delilah's lap for the climb back up to the mansion. She rarely read, or even looked at the mail during the ascent, but this day's delivery contained a formal-looking envelope. Wedding invitation. Graduation announcement.

She opened it as Nuncia and Dud pushed the chair slowly up the steepest part of the grade.

Dear Ms. Duncan,

It is with a very heavy heart that we write to inform you of the death of our daughter, Tara. She passed away last Tuesday after an overdose.

She spoke often of having met you, and of the many kindnesses you and the others at the hospital bestowed upon her. My husband and I want to offer our most sincere appreciation for your charity.

We are holding a ceremony in celebration of Tara's life on Saturday, March 17 at 1:00 PM at our church. The address is provided below. We would be honored if you could attend.

> *Again, many, many thanks.*
> *Mary and William Simms*

When they had entered the house, and after she had shared the letter with Nuncia and John Dudley, Delilah stood out of her wheelchair and placed her crutches around each forearm. She caned herself to the kitchen cabinet that contained liquor. Bottles of wine were always stacked in wooden racks on each side of the room, but she had stored the hard stuff out of sight. It was not good for her. Dobro had told her this a thousand times, and she knew it.

With some difficulty, she removed a bottle of brown liquor and held it precariously as she caned herself towards her bedroom.

"I really don't want to be bothered," she said as she inched herself away.

Nuncia and Dud busied themselves throughout the afternoon, but both were unsettled. They shared a genuine grief at the death of so bight a star as the girl they had known at the hospital; they were also terribly worried about Delilah.

At ten that evening, Delilah's door opened, and they could hear her caning her way toward the kitchen. Nuncia had been cleaning up after having prepared fried chicken and green beans. A plate containing healthy portions of both sat on the countertop sealed in plastic wrap.

"I saved you some dinner," she said as Delilah entered the room. "You must be hungry."

"Maybe in a minute," said Delilah. "Well, go ahead and heat it up if you don't mind. And can you get me a glass of water, please?"

Delilah had very clearly been drinking but seemed lucid.

"Are you alright?" asked John Dudley.

"I will be," she answered as she took a seat at the kitchen table. "Working?" she asked John.

His bible and several books of poetry were spread out in front of him.

"Just doing some work for the show."

"Good for you," she said. "I don't know if I've told you how proud I am of what you're doing. You have a real talent, Dud. I'm glad that we're doing this show."

"So am I," he said.

In actuality, he had grown to enjoy it. There was the obvious good he was able to do periodically, a caller here, a caller there. And there was the fact that his religious beliefs, every bit as fervent as the next person's, rankled Bruiser Butterman in that they extended beyond the Reverend's limited scope of understanding and inclusion. The priest knew good and well that his enjoyment of this fact was a sin. He also was very clearly of the mind that it was a sin that God Himself would smile at. And then, as a bit of icing on the cake, there were the bedtime visits from Nuncia that almost always occurred on nights of the show. These, in his mind, were not sins and he would not perform penance for enjoying them. All those years of celibacy had earned him these moments of comfort.

"I think we should go to the church thing for Tara," said Delilah. "It's possible that we could all burst into flame when we enter the building, but I say we risk it."

"The only one of us who's going to burn up will be me," said Nuncia.

"You're not going to burn up," said Delilah. "What are you doing that's so bad. Keeping Dud happy once in a while? Hell, that's kindness is all that is."

Dud's ears burned a bright red. Nuncia stopped on her way to deliver Delilah's dinner.

"You know about that?" she asked.

"Honey, when you've been laid as often as I have, you know it when you see it. Trust me."

John Dudley scratched his head and went back to the book of Taoist chants he had been reading.

"Is Dudley an Irish name?" asked Delilah without turning from her position in the front seat to face the priest.

They were on their way to the service for Tara. It was a chilly day for mid-March, with clouds threatening rain all morning.

"It is. I get it from both sides of my parents. My mother was all Irish."

"Do you ever do anything to celebrate St. Patrick's Day?"

"Not really. When I was a boy, sometimes an aunt or uncle would come to our house. They would sit around and drink what I'm assuming was whiskey, and they would listen to Irish music. But after my father died, that all stopped. My mother was never much of a drinker, despite being Irish."

"My father drinks like a fish," said Nuncia from the driver's seat. "But you know all about that."

"Same with my mother, may she rot in holy hell. But you know all about that, too."

Nuncia pulled the big SUV up to the front door of Saint Steven's, a mid-sized, well landscaped church with a red roof.

"Episcopals," said Dud.

"It's a church just like all the rest of them," said Nuncia. "What's the difference?"

"Not much, I'll give you that. We used to call the Episcopalian Church *Catholic Light*," he said as he got out of the back seat to open Delilah's door. "Everything pretty much the same as us, except they don't have the guilt."

"Tell us about it later, Father," said Delilah as she stepped down from her seat and wrapped the canes around her forearms. "I want to get in there and get a good seat. Somewhere near the front."

Dud accompanied Delilah into the entryway of Saint Steven's. There was a slanted table with a registration book, and each of them signed in.

"What address should I use," asked Dud.

"The only one you have," she answered.

They waited for Nuncia to join them after she had parked the car.

"We need to be a threesome when we go in," Delilah said.

The crowd was not large, consisting of twenty people or so. Delilah led the way up the aisle toward the altar and selected an empty pew for the three of them. She pointed one of her crutches to the opening.

"Here. This will do. You two go in first"

They were quiet for the first several minutes as they sat and waited for the service to begin.

"Why are there no young people?" Nuncia finally asked.

"They're possibly all dead," whispered Delilah. "If they were friends of hers, they may have done the same stuff as she did."

Moments later, a priest dressed in a black suit and black shirt entered from a door off the side of the altar area. He was tall and thin and walked with a dignity that seemed to come naturally. John Dudley watched him with sharp eyes. An athlete in his younger days he would have guessed. A star pupil who got all the girls.

The priest stood at the lectern from which he delivered sermons on Sunday mornings. He looked the crowd over and nodded; an orchestra leader tapping his baton to inform musicians that it was now time for a moment of silence before beginning.

"Brothers and sisters, thank you all for joining us on this cloudy St. Patrick's Day. We are here to gather informally at the request of Bill and Mary Simms to honor the life of their daughter Tara. Let us pray."

The Episcopalian priest chanted a prayer that Dudley recognized, and then another which he did not. From these recitations, he transitioned into a casual dialogue about the dangers of growing up in the world today. He touched on the trappings of young life, of the importance of strong families, of the comfort of knowing God. He was an excellent speaker, and he evoked both smiles and tears from those gathered in the pews in front of him. He did not go down the usual path of proclaiming that the day should be a happy one…the young girl now sitting with God and all of that. This logic had always seemed stupid to Dud… the loved ones of the departed were grieving for goodness sakes. How could they treat the day as anything other than twenty-four hours of misery? Grief was good, and Dud knew this. Let the mourners have their feelings, he thought. Don't insist that they ignore the obvious based on some arbitrary concept that they clearly would be unable to wrap their heads around. The Episcopalian priest also knew this. This was apparent to Dud, and it furthered his admiration of the man.

After a final prayer, the priest announced that Bill and Mary had arranged for refreshments to be served in the ante-room adjoining the church.

"Please join us for a cup of coffee and a sweet or two," he said. "Sorry for those of you wanting to celebrate St. Patrick's Day…nothing harder than that."

The congregation chuckled on cue and rose from the pews to move towards the room serving refreshments.

Bill and Mary Simms had positioned themselves at the entrance to the cookie room so as to greet those in attendance. They were impeccably dressed and stood with a tallness and strength that impressed each guest as they said their hellos and passed on into the room.

"I'm Delilah Duncan," Delilah said as she caned to a stop in front of them. "I was with your daughter for a bit at the hospital. She was a delightful young woman. I can't tell you how sorry I am for your loss."

"Thank you so much for coming," said Mary Simms. "Tara spoke of you all the time, how excited she was to meet such a big star, and of how kind you all were to her."

"We're big fans, by the way," said Tara's father. "We have all your records."

"That's kind," said Delilah. "These are two of my housemates," she said motioning with her head toward Nuncia and Dud behind her. "They knew Tara, as well. They live with me now."

Introductions completed, Delilah, Nuncia and Dud took seats off to the side of the room. Nuncia ladled red punch from a bowl into paper cups and delivered them, one-by-one, to her housemates.

"Anyone want a cookie? They're store-bought just in case you're wondering."

"I don't," said Delilah. "But listen. After things settle down in here and Tara's folks are making the rounds, I want you two to engage Tara's dad in some conversation. What was Tara like as a kid? You know, that kind of stuff? I want to talk to her mother alone."

After the crowd had begun to settle into seats positioned along the walls of the cookie room, Dud and Nuncia were directed by Delilah to seek out Tara's father. When they had reintroduced themselves and were standing in conversation with him, Delilah stood and caned her way towards Tara's mother.

"Again, how nice of you to come," said Mary Simms.

"I'm honored that you invited me. I hope it's all right that I brought along my sidekicks. They were very fond of your daughter."

Delilah deferred to an older man who stepped in to say his goodbyes to Mary. He proclaimed that he actually had another funeral to attend. Delilah looked at him with icy eyes as he left.

"Let me ask you something, Mary, if I may?"

Mary Simms' attention now focused back on the women in crutches, she smiled politely.

"Of course, Delilah. Anything."

"What does your husband do for a living? Tara mentioned on occasion how she came from such a perfect and loving family...you should know that...and I was just wondering what Mr. Simms did."

"He's an attorney," said Mary Simms. "Partner in a small firm."

"That's good to know," said Delilah. "I need attorneys from time to time when I need to get myself out of trouble."

She smiled at herself.

"Well, Bill won't do you any good, I'm afraid. His firm handles mostly real estate. I'm not sure he would be much help in getting you out of trouble."

"I'm kidding," said Delilah. "I live just about the most boring life imaginable. I was just curious."

Dud was silent for the entire ride back to the mansion. Nuncia attempted to draw him out, but he was sullen. He looked out the window from the center of the back seat.

"What's the matter with you?" Nuncia asked when they had returned to Delilah's house and were sitting alone at the kitchen table.

"I'm fine," he said. "I'm going to go do some reading."

"No, you are not, mister priest. Something is eating you and I want to know what it is."

"Okay, I'll share with you. I was just a little bit in awe of that priest at the Episcopalian Church is all. He was so smooth, and he just seemed to know exactly what to say.

I was never, on my best day, as...I don't know the word... *accomplished* as he was. I don't think I ever realized until just today what a crappy priest I probably was. I mean in general."

Nuncia exhaled loudly and placed her hand over Dud's.

"You were probably a better priest than you think, Dud. That guy today was older than you. He's just had more time to practice all the priesty stuff, you know?"

He nodded. She knew this had helped a touch.

"And I'll tell you something else, mister Dud. I'll bet that that priest today doesn't have a cock as big as yours."

At this he smiled.

"You're really something, Nuncia. You really are."

"Dobro, it's Delilah. I hate to bother you at home. You busy?"

"Never too busy for you, Delilah. What's going on?"

"First, thanks for handling that whole Jon thing. I could have done it, but it's just so much easier when you do those kinds of things."

"That's why you pay me, Delilah. Although in his case, that would have been a freebie. I was never crazy about that guy. He was pretty resigned to his fate at the end of our conversation. I'm pretty sure he knew it was coming. How did he go out?"

"With a whimper," said Delilah. "He was just gone the next morning. I figured he'd need a ride or something. But he just vanished."

"He knew his severance was on the line if he made any kind of a scene. How's the radio show going?" asked Dobro.

He was sitting on the deck of his house in Topanga. The house was all beams and glass and was set halfway up a hill, surrounded by trees. He wore the usual pair of jeans, but his feet were bare, and he wasn't wearing a shirt.

"It's a fucking hit, if you can even believe that. My priest is so uncomfortable it almost makes it good. He's gone from having to read bible stuff to fill dead air to not being able to take all the calls that come in during the hour."

"I'm curious, Delilah. What kind of calls is he getting?"

"At first, they all seemed to be about not believing in God anymore. Now, though, they're all over the place. Abortion, gay people, assisted suicide, is my dead father in heaven or hell? You name it, Dobro, he seems to get it."

"Does he give good advice?"

"Pretty much the same advice for everyone. *Pray about it.* Even if you don't believe in God, or even if you have different Gods than everyone else, just pray. He tells them that maybe something good will happen, just from forming the words. Almost like a mantra, or something like that. Maybe they'll figure some stuff out. And he always asks them to call back in. He's very genuine, Dobro. He really is. He's honest, and these callers pick up on that."

"Any trouble with The Reverend?"

"No. He wants to sell ad space during the show. He tells me that I can make a lot of money if he does, but I wonder if that wouldn't just pollute the whole thing. I don't know. I'll give it some thought. I might have to have you call him."

"Just let me know," said Dobro.

"Oh, and you'll like this, my priest schools the shit out of The Reverend. Like The Reverend will use some quote from the bible and John corrects him. 'That's not what that says, Reverend.' And then he'll recite the proper lines and explain it to the stupid asshole. The Reverend challenged him a few times…got out his own bible to check…but now he's almost never there during the show anymore. And if he is, he doesn't say word one."

"Nice," said Dobro. "So, what can I do for you, Delilah? I hate it, but I have to run out shortly. A client's kid's birthday party. I have to make an appearance. See the pony delivered. But you come first. What's up?"

"I need you to very discretely find somebody for me."

"I don't like the way this is starting to make me feel," he said. "Let me go inside and get a notepad."

Delilah gave him the abridged version of the life and death of Tara Simms.

"So, it isn't bad enough that this monster was probably having sex with this teenage girl…you should have seen her, Dobro, she was just sparkling…but he has to go ahead and get her going on smack."

"Why no cops?" asked Dobro.

"She didn't know why not. This was her father's business partner at some law firm. Her suspicion was that she would have been dragged through the mud and that nothing would happen in the end. That this guy was fucking some underage girl, well, remember that we're in the south, Dobro. This isn't Topanga Canyon, buddy."

After Delilah had provided as much detail as she possessed on who the man might be: the name of the firm, the approximate time of his departure, a rough guess as to his age, Dobro flipped his notepad onto the coffee table in his living room.

"Say I'm able to find this guy," he said, "say I hire someone to do some digging and we locate him…which shouldn't be that hard, now that I'm thinking about it…what are you going to do with that information? This kind of shit scares me to death, Delilah."

"I just want to know," she said. "And you know me, Dobro. If there's anything even slightly dirty about anything that needs to be done, I have you on speed dial."

Dobro called three weeks later with the news. Delilah went to her room and closed the door.

"I have his name and address and where he works. I even have the church he goes to."

"I knew I could count on you, Dobro. You never fail to amaze me."

"Years of taking care of people who seem to be able to afford almost any indulgence life might offer," he said. "So, what's the plan, now that you know who this scumbag is?"

"I hate it that he got away so free and easy with all of this. I mean, having sex with a teenager is one thing. But the drug stuff. That's hard for me to process. What's he doing now?"

"He got out of the law biz, and now he sells real estate. Small houses. No big ticket items."

"What if we did up a letter...untraceable...telling everything that happened. We do up the timeline of him seducing this beautiful girl, the daughter of his business partner, for God sakes, and then getting her into heroin. Oh, and infecting her with a venereal disease. And we send this letter to all these people, anonymously, of course, to all these people. The cops, all the television stations in the area, this bastard's church. And we just see what happens."

There was a pause from Dobro's end. Delilah knew him well enough to picture his feet on the table in front of him. She could see the seriousness of his demeanor as he processed what she had just suggested. Biting the side of his cheek, furrowing his brow.

"Alright, Delilah, I'll do what you want me to do, and you know that. But hear me out on something first, okay?"

"I'm all ears," she said.

"This guy is scum," he said. "I get that and, you know better than most, I have no difficulty taking care of scum."

Delilah thought back to the endgame with her mother. The investigation Dobro had conducted was so detailed, the judge handling the case had to be convinced by Delilah's attorney and a social worker that it would not have been in the best interest of the then-twenty- year old up-and-rising rock star to push it into criminal court once they were done. Delilah's mother left the room penniless and with no place to live. The rest of her short life was not pretty. There were gigs in low-budget porno films, there was prostitution. But Dobro made certain to keep those details from his young client. He'd gone so far as to pay off the tabloids that might well have run the story of the star's mother's destitute and sorrowful last days.

"I'm going to ask you to think about a couple of things," he resumed. "First, once these letters hit, the first door that's going to get knocked on is her parents'. You have to ask yourself if we should be making that decision for them. There was a reason they didn't blow the whistle on this guy when it happened. Maybe to protect the daughter…to protect Tara. But maybe additional reasons. We have to ask ourselves if we know enough about their reasoning to over-rule it. That's one thing," he said.

She was sitting side-saddle on her bed. Her right arm rested on her lap, barely moving.

"What else?" she said.

"You need to know that the guy has rounded the corner on his addiction. By all accounts, and believe me, Delilah, I was thorough, he has gotten his act together. I'm not saying he needs to be forgiven, and if Tara was my daughter, I might not be talking this way, but maybe we want to talk about our own karma. This letter of yours sure as shit will mess up the guy's life. But what do you get out of that, Delilah? It would be nice to see all the scumbags in the world get what's coming to them, but we don't know the demons this guy battles. Just think about the fact that he might suffer on a daily basis for what he did. That's all I'm saying."

Dobro waited through the seconds of silence. He placed the legal pad that had been resting on his lap back on his table. He knew what she was going to say before she did.

"You're right, of course," she said. "Mostly, it's not fair to the parents. I met them. They're stand-up people, and they're grieving right now. You're a hundred percent right, Dobro. Thank you for your advice and for your friendship."

"I do it 'cause you pay me, Delilah. You know that."

This, along with a genuine sense of relief at having changed her mind, made her smile.

"There is one thing I think we should do," she said.

"What's that?"

"I think we should somehow make sure this guy knows that Tara died. He needs to own a piece of that."

Dobro sat silently and looked out the window. He had orchestrated far more chilling attempts at arbitrary justice than this. And he also knew that in each of these instances the gratification was never equal to the guilt.

"Never mind," said Delilah, "you're just going to talk me out of that one, too, aren't you?"

"Send me a tape of the priest's show," he said. "I'd love to have a listen."

Dobro Temple was perceptive in most areas of his life. He possessed many strengths in understanding people, primarily his clients. But it was his ability to recognize when it was time to run quickly away from a conversation when a doorway briefly presented itself that kept him on top of the game.

"I thought long and hard about whether to share something with you."

Millie sat in her usual chair in the candle-lit room inside The Garden of Healing. On this day, she wore loose fitting sweatpants and a bright yellow tank top. Her feet, as almost always, were bare. Before sitting, she had selected a fire red crystal. She held it in her lap and fondled it like a child would a new toy.

"And I can tell by that statement that you probably decided to go ahead, right? Please, share."

Meryl sat in the well-indented crater her rather prodigious rear end had created in her half of the sofa over the past several months of counseling. The other half of the couch was flat, and the disparity, now obvious each time she entered the room, had begun to bother her. A new piece of furniture was going to be needed, and relatively soon.

"I had sex with my Art Professor," said Millie.

"Well, that is just about the last thing I would have guessed you would be telling me today," said Meryl. "Can I ask what prompted it?"

"I can't answer that. Believe me, I've been hashing this over since it happened. It happened last week. I have no earthly idea why I did it. I went to his office to apologize for kissing him in the parking lot. It was all going according to plan, you know. Then I left his office and got to the stairwell."

Millie paused here as if to repaint the scene accurately in her memory before going on.

"I just turned around and went back to his office. I closed the door and locked it, and we did it."

Meryl wanted to ask the right questions. She wanted to ask the questions that would, when Millie answered them, allow for some insights. She wanted to ask questions that would lead Millie to a better understanding of her actions. She wanted dialogue that would guide her client to a moment of clarity.

But more than that, she wanted details. She had been living somewhat vicariously through the beautiful young Korean woman and her dashing psychiatrist husband. Meryl's ten minute sessions of near nakedness, lying on the couch under her blanket had become standard operating procedure following every session with Millie. She secretly looked forward to her own session more than those with Millie.

"Was that easily accomplished there in his office?" she asked.

"Pretty easy," said Millie with an air of nonchalance. "I took off my shoes and my pants, and he bent me over his desk and did it. There were papers everywhere...all over the floor."

"Let me ask you, Millie, were you worried about getting caught?"

"I should have been worried about a lot of things, but I just seemed to be moving on auto-pilot, you know. It was almost an out-of-body kind of experience. I was aware of what was happening. I was aware that he was inside me and everything. I could feel all of that. It was just that it almost seemed like he was doing this with someone else. Does that make any sense at all?"

Meryl knew it was her turn to talk, but she needed a moment to collect herself. The image of her client bent over the professor's desk was almost more than she could handle. The crystal in her lap, a yellow one, was getting a workout.

"Was it pleasurable? Let me rephrase...did you go ahead with this out of some sense of seeking pleasure? Do you think that might be it?"

Millie placed the red crystal she had been holding on the table separating her chair with Meryl's couch. She folded her hands in her lap.

"No. I mean, Edward and I have a very good physical relationship. He's a wonderful lover. He's the most attentive man I've ever been around. So it wasn't that. It wasn't pleasure I went there looking for."

"What do you think it was? What might have caused you to go there that afternoon?"

Millie took a deep breath, the deepest of her life. She had been raised in a family that derived enormous pride from their collective ability to process unexpected developments rationally. Emotion was never a first option and was to be harnessed always.

Meryl saw her eyes fill with tears.

"Here," she said as she tossed a box of tissues into Millie's lap.

Millie dabbed each eye with a folded corner of a tissue and placed the box on the table next to her crystal.

"Thanks," she said. "Punishment. I think I went there to punish someone."

"Have you thought about who you were trying to punish?"

Millie looked at Meryl with just a tinge of coldness in her eyes. This was different, this was new, and this was unsettling to Meryl.

"You think? You think I've given any thought to that, Meryl?"

"So, who?"

"Probably myself," she said. "For being a shitty wife once in a while, for pushing back every time Edward wants to talk about having another baby, for growing a little bit apart from this man who loves me. And it was safe with David. Other than his knowledge of art and all of that, he holds no appeal for me. He's not that handsome. He's not really very interesting. It was safe. I used him, that's all. Jesus Christ, he's *shorter* than me."

"How was this punishing yourself?"

"If you knew the kind of family I was raised in, what kind of perfect young Korean girl I was raised to be, you'd see how this was self-immolation almost…without the flames. I'll beat myself up for a long time over what I did, believe me."

"Do you think you'll see him again? I mean, in some capacity other than your class with him?"

Millie smiled.

"I'm not going back. I mean, who am I kidding? What am I going to do with an undergraduate degree in Art History, anyway? This was just killing time. All this thinking I've been doing about what happened, at least I came to that realization."

"What are you going to do, Millie?"

"I don't know, but I have no doubt that whatever it is, it will be meaningful."

When Millie Chase had left The Garden of Healing, Meryl sat in the chair her client had just occupied. Despite the titillating subject matter of the session she had just had, she was not tempted to act out what had become the usual ten minutes of self-gratification that followed sessions with Millie. Masturbation, Meryl knew, was often associated with depression. And she was not depressed.

Meryl had gone into counseling to help people. Although her intentions had been pure from the outset, she often questioned her abilities. She had learned several tricks of the trade, had developed the skill set, of course. She had her crystals and her candles. But the application of these skills in a manner that would allow people to heal themselves was never something she truly thought herself capable of.

As she sat in the semi-darkness and stared at the indented sofa cushion across from her, she mulled over Millie's last statement.

"It will be meaningful," she had said. "It will be meaningful."

Meryl didn't know much, but she suspected that Millie Chase, at the end of this session, was in a far better place than she had probably been in since her first visit. Meryl was comforted by this thought. This was success, or, at the very least, something close to success.

"I just don't know how you are allowed to preach such crap about our Lord Jesus Christ. I can't believe some part of that radio station…and I've been listening to the Reverend Bruiser for a long time now…I don't understand how you are given this flexibility to lie about this stuff the way you are."

This was a caller late into the hour-long time slot. Although The Reverend had no editorial control over the subject matter of John Dudley's radio show, he had very secretly instructed the station's call-screener to hold calls with the potential of becoming argumentative to the end of the hour. His assumption was that the show might end on a down note, that the priest might be painted in colors that called his own authority into question.

"What am I lying about, caller?" Dud calmly asked the man.

"All this hocus pocus about the world being billions of years old. All this undiluted crap about evolution, about people evolving out of apes. I don't listen to this show very often because it makes me sick to my stomach. Don't you read Genesis? Don't you believe in the word of God? That He created the universe in seven days and not billions of years."

"Well, in actuality, it says it took six days. On the seventh day He rested, right?"

"You keep telling these people who call into your show the same garbage. And I got news for you."

"Caller, we're running short on time. Can you tell me what news you have for me in thirty seconds?"

"I can tell you in shorter time than that. You're going to hell, young man. You're going to burn in hell with the other sinners and blasphemers who call into this show. And that's what I'm going to pray for, you Godless pig."

Dud took a deep breath, audible to the entirety of his listening audience.

"I guess on that note we'll take one last break," he said.

The call screener, a boy working the board at WGOD part time as he was completing his last year of high school, and whose own spiritual beliefs had been transformed from almost militant to more mainstream and all-encompassing, held the chalkboard up to the window.

Nice composure!

Dud smiled as he read it and looked at his notes for a parting comment before going off the air. Then, another note from the boy in the control room.

One last call. Said he needs to talk to you!

"Okay, listeners. It looks like we may have just enough time for one last call. Caller, please make it quick if you can."

"I haven't been in a fight in a long time," said the voice on the other end of the line," but if you want me to, I'll find that guy who was just on the line and straighten him out. If you want me to."

Dud looked through the window and into the control room to the kid running the board, and then to the matching Jesus portraits.

"I think I know you," he said into his microphone. "I think I know you from a place we were both visiting a couple months ago."

"You do," said the voice. "I know no last names on the show, so I'll just tell you my name is Peter. Do you remember me?"

Dudley smiled and scratched his head.

"Of course, I do. I have been praying for you. Of course, I remember you. How have you been?"

The silence that permeated the air waves was palpable. Five seconds felt like fifty to the priest.

"Your prayers are working," said Peter. "I've been doing okay. Staying out of trouble. Working. Day by day, just like we used to talk about. I kind of stumbled on your show here, and I just wanted to tell you that I was doing alright. Not perfect, but the best I can. I think so, anyway."

Dud smiled widely; his teeth bared as a toothpaste model.

"Then God has found a path to you, my friend. It's all Him, but you deserve a lot of credit for hanging in there for as long as it took. Forget about all that crap the previous caller was going on and on about. That's only his own insecurity talking. None of that is important. What is important is that you are on your way now. To where, I can't tell you. But you're moving, you're processing, You're making efforts to understand. And all of this is being done in God's light, Peter. Oh my, but it's good to hear your voice."

"Just wanted to call and check in, man," said Peter.

"Please stay on the line so that I can get your information," said Dud, "and don't go beating up the poor man who called in before you."

The segment ran forty-five seconds over its allotted time. The boy running the board was certain that he would be receiving a call from Bruiser about the error. He was also well-aware that Bruiser would ask how the hell he could have put on another call after the fire-and-brimstone oration. In the end, he really didn't care. This was a part-time job that paid him minimum wage. And he was genuinely growing to love the word of God and His teachings as espoused by John Dudley. The Reverend Robert "Bruiser" Butterman could go to hell.

That evening, after Nuncia had served a dinner of braised lamb shanks and horseradish mashed potatoes, she sat at the kitchen table with Delilah.

"I almost can't remember the last time we sat in the dining room," she said.

"This is homey," said Delilah as she sipped red wine from a juice glass. "And we can keep our eye on the radio star over there. Make sure he doesn't cut any corners washing up."

This had become evening ritual. Nuncia cooked and served, Delilah ate and drank expensive wines, John Dudley cleared the dishes after dinner and cleaned the kitchen.

"How crazy is it that that boy Peter called into the radio show today?" said Nuncia.

"I was sitting right here," said Delilah. "I had just made myself a cup of tea and had parked my ass right here in this seat. I almost turned the show off. I knew it was just about time for Dud to sign off. I'm so glad I kept listening."

"He's driving a truck," said Dud from the sink. "His uncle owns a fruit and vegetable business in Roanoke. Peter delivers stuff all over the valley. He sounded pretty good, I think."

"You win some, you lose some," said Nuncia. "I think about Tara a lot. That was one we definitely lost."

When the dishes had been loaded into the dishwasher, when the pots and pans Nuncia had used to prepare their dinner were scoured, dried and put away and when the counter and stove tops had been wiped clean, John Dudley said his goodnights to the women still seated at the table off to the side. It had been a long day. The days of his show exhausted him. He no longer stayed awake throughout the nights before broadcast; he had almost conditioned himself to relax just before and during airtime. But he refused to go into the tiny studio without having prepared sufficiently to fill dead air in the event no one called in. At this point in the show's run that would be unlikely. The boy handling the phone lines and the audio board typically turned callers away as the end of the hour approached. But Dud wanted to have a back-up plan, just in case.

He was tired, but not nearly as tired as his affectations suggested. It had been a long day, but not longer than usual. He wanted to brush his teeth and climb into his bed not simply in search of a good night's sleep. It was show night, and he knew that there was a good possibility he would be visited in his bed.

An hour after climbing into bed, he lay reading. On the nights after having done his show, he skipped the formality of wearing pajamas. He loved the way Nuncia's dark skin felt against his as she climbed in beside him. This was pleasure; this was not sin.

She knocked lightly on the door before opening it and entering the priest's room.

"You want me to come in, Dud?"

"I do. For sure," he said.

He watched her undress and catalogued the images of her body as each one was revealed. The darkness of her up-turned nipples, the flat stomach, the triangle of pubic hair, her long legs, he smallish feet. When she climbed in beside him, he breathed in the air she brought to him.

"Before we do this, before we get going, I need to tell you something," she said.

He had placed his hand on her belly and now pulled it instinctively back.

"Okay," he said. "Everything alright, Nuncia?"

"Yes. I guess," she said.

She was silent, and Dud did not want to interrupt the moment. He was filled with a combination of eagerness and anxiousness.

"You know what happens when people do this, right?" she asked. "I mean, they teach you in the priest school what happens when people do this sex thing, don't they, Dud?"

He swallowed hard in an effort to push his heart back to its normal resting place and out of his throat.

"Yes," he said a squeaky voice any listener would have associated with pre-pubescence.

"Well, Mr. Priest, that's what's happened. I'm sorry. I didn't even think about it very much. Once in a while I'd think about using something. Maybe it's because you're a priest. I didn't think anything could happen from a priest."

"I don't know what to say," he said. Her head rested in the crook of his large arm. She spoke into his chest, he toward the ceiling.

"You don't have to say anything," she said. "And I'm only telling you because you have a right to know. I don't want you to feel like you have to do anything. I will take care of everything. I will raise her up and take care of all the details, Dud."

"But that's not what I want," he said. "I don't have a clue how to be a good father, but that's what I want to be. Should we get married, Nuncia? Should I marry you?"

"You know, Dud, for a pretty smart man that was a really stupid question. Of course, we should not get married. That would just get in the way of things right now."

"I'm going to take care of you," he said. "I'll take care of you and the baby. You watch. I'll do it."

She smiled at this. What had begun on a dare, having sex with this man simply because no one had done so before, had grown into real and restless desire for Nuncia. Her sexual background was, at best, limited and under-explored. Not that sex with the priest was anything earth-shattering. But she was comfortable with him. He was gentle and he listened to her as she helped him find his way from place to place.

When they had finished, Nuncia rolled off the large man and resumed her resting place nestled into his chest.

"Have you thought about hurting yourself anymore, since we got out of the hospital and moved in here with Delilah?" she asked.

"Yes," he said. "I have thought about it. But not now. Not after hearing from Peter today, and not after hearing that we're going to have a baby."

"I have, too," she said. "These things just don't fly away once you get out of the hospital, do they? It's not like we're suddenly cured of everything that ate us, you know?"

"I love you," he said.

It was the first time he had spoken those words to anyone other than his mother.

"Let's not complicate the whole thing, Dud. I won't tell you that I *don't* love you, but that's all I can give you right now. Let's just raise this little girl up the best we can and see where the dust settles on us. Okay, Dud."

He smiled. The tiny idiosyncrasies that seemed to attach themselves to Nuncia's English always made him smile.

"How do you know it's a girl?" he asked into the darkness.

"I just know," she said. "It is."

Dud lingered in his bed for an extra hour the next morning. He wanted to make sure Delilah had eaten her breakfast of wheat toast and fresh slices of fruit. He wanted to wait until after she had plopped into her easy chair in the windows of the living room looking out over the horse farms across the valley.

"May I speak to you for a minute?" he asked.

"Sure. I was thinking that you might want to chat with me," she said.

Delilah pushed the cushion she had been resting her feet and ankles on away from her chair. She motioned for Dud to sit on it.

"Has Nuncia talked to you?"

"Yup. I didn't know you had it in you, Father Dud. How do you feel about that?"

"Terrified," he said. "But resolved."

"That's what she told me. That's good. She's so fucking independent. I'm glad that you have the balls to hang in there. It'll be a real positive that you'll be there for her, Dud."

"I need to talk to you about that," he said. "I've been thinking, and I think I need to quit doing the show."

"How come?" asked Delilah. "We love the show. *People* love the show."

"I'll need to be getting a real job, Delilah. What you've provided us, that you've welcomed us into your home, has been one of the greatest kindnesses I've ever witnessed. I cannot tell you how grateful we are, how grateful I am. But I need to make a living. I've never been in this position before, but I need to be a breadwinner. Somehow, some way, I need to think about security for Nuncia and this baby."

Delilah took all this in. She looked directly into the priest's eyes and then back across the valley. As she had grown through middle age and begun to inch along the short pathway towards being an older woman, there had been no challenge she had encountered that could not resolve simply by throwing money at it. Her independence and strength of character were undeniable assets. But her bank account tipped the scales in her favor one hundred present of the time. A feather opposite a bowling ball.

"You're a nice man," she finally said to Dud. "Go fetch me the phone."

Her arm, resting in her lap, was motionless.

"Stay here," she said to Dud as she picked up the phone. "I want you to hear this."

After she had apologized for calling him so early and at home, she explained the situation to Dobro. And after she had given him instructions to direct the radio station to begin to sell airtime to advertisers and to pay Dud a salary, she waved the priest away.

"Just give me a minute alone with Dobro," she said. "Get Nuncia. I need to talk to both of you in a few minutes."

"I've got that," said Dobro. "What else is up, Delilah? You're good with all this, right?"

"I'm more than good, Dobro. You taking notes?"

"You know I am."

"Okay, a couple of things, and they're not negotiable. One, I want the mansion put in their names. I'll send you the details. Two, I want a trust fund set up for that baby. Not a huge amount, but a comfortable amount. Maybe half a mil or something along those lines. You decide. Three, we need to get these two some insurance. Maybe form a company or something, make them employees. You figure it out. You getting all this, Dobro? I don't want to have to repeat myself."

"I know that this is not negotiable, Delilah. I heard that loud and clear. I'm just going to ask you one question. You sure about all of this? I mean, once they own the mansion, they can evict you for Christ sakes."

"I'm about as fucking sure of this as I've ever been of anything in my life, Dobro, but I appreciate you asking. They're not going to evict anybody, and so what if they do. I'll just buy another place. No biggie, Dobro. Now, let's get cracking, shall we?"

Dobro flipped the legal pad back on to his table before he hung the phone up. Just when he had allowed himself to believe that there would be no more surprises out of this woman in Virginia, along came this latest laundry list of action items.

He thought back to the moment he had decided to take her on as a client. She was young, and tight, and beautiful. She possessed a voice that was simply too big to be coming out of that young girl's body. She exuded sex-appeal and innocence in equal portions. She had the potential to earn millions of dollars.

But she was saddled, crippled by a mother whose sole intention was to feed her own, selfish wants. Delilah suffered greatly as a result of this woman's indifference. As if it was not enough that this woman ignored any sense of maternal responsibility, she had used her position of confidence with Delilah to feed her own indulgences. Delilah was forced to watch her mother go down the path of more men, more drugs, more money. Not only had Delilah been forced to witness all of this. She'd had to pay for it.

And it was at this moment, at this time of desperation, that Dobro had agreed to take on the young star. He'd been there for all of it ever since. The huge fame and money that came her way, the eventual but inevitable downward slide to has-been status, the physical decline, the faked disease, the alcohol abuse and subsequent trips to rehab facilities and mental hospitals. Through all of this, he had remained loyal. His interest, almost exclusively, was in her wellbeing.

He sat and looked out the window at the forest of trees surrounding his home in the hills. He was tempted to worry. His client had just directed him to transfer a ton of wealth from her own name into the names of two people he had never met. Delilah could be extravagant, but this was very clearly over the top.

But Dobro Temple did not worry. He was able to remember the level of commitment a young Delilah Duncan had displayed as she looked to develop her career. Her focus, her ambition, her energy were all there in prodigious amounts. As he thought back to moments earlier, to the sound of her voice as she explained the need to take care of these two people he did not know and the baby they had produced, he felt the essence of Delilah's ambition to succeed in this, her latest quest. He had not heard that voice in many years. It washed over him like light. It made him smile.

Millie and Edward

Millie was standing barefoot in her kitchen. She had just taken porkchops which had been marinating out of the refrigerator and placed them on the counter. Her plan was to grill them after Edward had got home and they had gone for a walk, their nightly ritual.

She had decided not to return to Weatherly. She was not intimidated or nervous at the thought of seeing David again; there simply seemed no point to it. Edward had shrugged it off. It was, in his mind, purely her decision. She had not yet informed her parents that their daughter seemed now destined to go through life without a college degree.

After Edward had arrived and changed into his shorts and sandals, they walked the cul-de-sac out to the main road and back. With two driveways to go before their own, she took his hand in hers.

"Let's go away for the weekend. Maybe to that place in the mountains again. That was fun."

"And the food was really good," he said. "I'll arrange it."

"Hey, Edward. I want to ask you something."

"What, Mil?"

"You know how you used to always bug the shit out of me to get a new car? Is that offer still on the table? Could we go car-shopping?"

"Of course, we can," he said. "We can go tomorrow after work if you like. We could get you a new car and you could drive it on the trip this weekend if you'd like."

True to his word, Edward arrived home earlier than normal the next evening. They drove Millie's old Honda to the Mercedes dealership on the outskirts of town. It took one test drive and approximately thirty minutes for the deal to be completed. Millie's new car was black and shiny and spoke to a woman who was very clearly of substance.

Two days later, a Friday, Edward pulled into the driveway just after three in the afternoon. They were headed to the mountains as soon as he could pack a bag. Millie was going to drive her new car.

"I'm not bringing any fancy clothes," he said from the bedroom. "I'd really love to stay completely casual, if that's alright with you."

"That's perfect," she said. "I'm on the same wavelength."

She stood in their bathroom, a small leather bag on the counter beside her sink. She wrapped her toothbrush in toilet paper and placed it, along with a tube of toothpaste, in the opened bag. She opened the drawer to the side of the basin and removed the round, plastic container that contained her birth control pills. She opened the container and inspected the tiny tablets, one for each day of the month. She was one week in.

She leaned forward and looked directly into the eyes of the woman in the mirror. She almost smiled at herself but the moment seemed too serious for smiles.

Before zipping her travel bag closed, she replaced the pill container in the drawer and shut it gently.

"You almost ready, Edward?" she said as she took one last glance into the mirror in front of her.

Author's Note

This is a work of fiction. All of the characters have been created. Obviously, Cass Elliot and David Bowie are real, but I was never blessed with an opportunity to meet them, and I know nothing of them. Except for their greatness. They are mentioned in this book merely for context.

My only genuine rubbing of elbows with a celebrity was the evening I got to dance with Mary McDonough who, as a young girl, played Erin Walton on the television show *The Waltons*. I'm reluctant to say much about this encounter but I hope that my dance partner from those many years ago remembers the evening with as much enjoyment as I do.

Lastly, this book deals somewhat peripherally with the subjects of mental illness and suicide. It is my great hope that, in the event anyone reading this might or could be helped with professional care, that he or she reach out for it. And know that Father John Dudley is somewhere out there pulling for you.

Printed in the United States
by Baker & Taylor Publisher Services